PL 260-1997
Fund 191

Searching for Atticus

Searching for Atticus

JAN MARINO

Simon & Schuster Books for Young Readers

Other books by Jan Marino

EIGHTY-EIGHT STEPS TO SEPTEMBER

THE DAY THAT ELVIS CAME TO TOWN

LIKE SOME KIND OF HERO

FOR THE LOVE OF PETE

THE MONA LISA OF SALEM STREET

SIMON & SCHUSTER BOOKS FOR YOUNG READERS
An imprint of Simon & Schuster Children's Publishing Division
1230 Avenue of the Americas, New York, New York 10020
Text copyright © 1997 by Jan Marino
SIMON & SCHUSTER BOOKS FOR YOUNG READERS is a trademark of Simon & Schuster.
Book design by Lucille Chomowicz
The text of this book is set in Stone Serif.
Printed and bound in the United States of America
First Edition
10 9 8 7 6 5 4 3 2 1
Library of Congress Cataloging-in-Publication Data
Marino, Jan. Searching for Atticus / Jan Marino   p.   cm.
Summary: As she tries to help her father deal with his memories of Vietnam,
fifteen-year-old Tess finds comfort in her friendship with the sensible Selina
and distraction in her infatuation with the dangerous Caleb.
ISBN 0-689-80066-5 (hardcover)
[1. Fathers and daughters-Fiction. 2. Post-traumatic stress disorder-Fiction.
3. Interpersonal relations-Fiction.]
I. TitlePZ.M33884Sej 1997
[Fic]-dc21 96-53146
CIP AC

For Irene DeBenedictis Marino
and Stephanie Owens Lurie
with thanks and love

❖   ❖   ❖

And in memory of my beloved friends
Pam and Fred

Chapter One

When I was little I used to fantasize that I was in an accident, or had a horrible disease, and was taken to the hospital. My father's hospital. He would come rushing over to me, tears running down his cheeks, and tell me everything would be all right. He would say that he was sorry for not spending more time with me. That from now on we would go on picnics and take long walks. That things would be different. But I never had that accident, and I was never that sick.

As I got older I got used to my father not spending much time with me. Most of the kids I knew also had fathers who traveled or were always busy. I began to think that was just the way fathers were. Until I met Clio.

Clio came to our school in fifth grade and instantly became the most popular girl in the class. Her father owned a movie theater in downtown Milwaukee, and being friends with Clio meant you got to go to the movies free. I guess in the beginning that was one of the reasons Clio and I got friendly, but it wasn't the only reason. I really liked her. And her father. Her mother was okay, but kind of snobby. It was her father who was special.

It was funny. My father looked exactly like Gregory Peck, the actor who played Atticus Finch in *To Kill a Mockingbird,* a movie that Clio and I saw about a hundred times. He was tall, with black hair always falling across his face, and penetrating dark eyes. But it was Clio's father who acted like Atticus. I remember sitting in the dark, watching Gregory Peck, thinking that if my father owned a movie theater, or if he wasn't a surgeon always on call, he might have been a father like Atticus Finch. I remember getting teary every time I watched the end of the movie. The part where Atticus goes into Jem's room while Jem is unconscious, his arm all done up in a cast, and sits beside the bed until Jem wakes up the next morning.

One day I told my mother how I felt. She listened, as she always did, then told me how different people love in different ways. She said that being a surgeon drained my father at times, but he loved us very much. But it wasn't the way Clio's father loved her, the way Atticus loved Jem and Scout, the way I wanted to be loved.

Just before I turned thirteen, my father went to Vietnam. He didn't have to go. He volunteered.

When my mother raised a fuss about his going, telling him he was too old at forty-seven to be doing such a thing, he told her he was needed there, that some of the kids he had operated on were now serving over there. "They need me," he'd said.

I wanted to tell him I needed him, my mother needed him, but I knew telling him wouldn't change anything.

When he left for Vietnam, my mother missed him, I knew that. So did I. I really did. I missed him padding around the house in his slippers, the ones with the backs caved in. Or peering into the refrigerator to see what my mother and I had had for dinner. But I had to admit the house seemed lighter. No frantic phone calls from anxious parents, no sick kids lined up in the waiting room, some of them wandering from his office into the main house.

My mother seemed lighter, too. She played her Big Band music. She never did that when my father was home. She always said he needed the peace and quiet he found in Bach.

One time, when my father had been gone almost a year, she even went out with my father's best friend. It wasn't exactly a date. Dr. Olney and his wife invited her to go to the hospital benefit party as their guest, but then Mrs. Olney came down with shingles and couldn't go. At first my mother said she couldn't go, but then, at the last minute, she decided if people gossiped about her being alone with Dr. Olney, that was their problem.

I remember her that night—the way she looked, the way she acted. Almost like she was my age, she was that excited. Dr. Olney brought the corsage he'd bought for his wife and pinned it on her. I swear she looked like she was going to her high school prom. All that next day she kept telling me how wonderful the party had been. "I felt like Cinderella," she said. "It would have been absolutely perfect if your father had been there."

All the while my father was away, we wrote to him almost every day. He wrote back whenever he could. Short letters, telling us he was fine, and not to worry. That he missed us. My mother's letters went on and on. She'd tell him what was happening at the clinic, where she worked as a nurse practitioner. Who was ready to deliver. Who had delivered.

Then she always tried to get me to tell him what was going on in my life.

This time was no different.

"Tell him about the girls blaming you for failing the waltz."

"He doesn't want to hear any of that."

"Come on, Tess, tell him. We need to tell him even the little things we're doing." She passed me the piece of nearly transparent stationery she always wrote on. "You'll see. He's going to come back a changed man, I know it. War does funny things to people. Makes them more aware of what's important."

And so I wrote about Miss Otis, my gym teacher, forcing me to play the "Skater's Waltz" on the piano for every girl who had to pass her "Waltzing Course." Everybody who didn't pass told Miss Otis I hadn't played in three-quarter time. "Nonsense. Your failing had nothing to do with Tess's timing. Is it her timing that makes you hold your partner like you're in the boxing ring? Her timing that makes you do a fox-trot instead of a waltz?"

Before my mother sealed the letter, she tucked a piece of cotton sprinkled with perfume into the envelope.

"There," she said, smiling. "I'll just bet we get some letters soon."

We didn't, not for weeks. And when one finally came, my mother didn't tear it open the way she always did. She turned it over and over, then held it to her lips.

"Hurry up," I said. "Open it."

When she finally did, a smile spread across her face. "He's coming home, Tess."

"When?"

She held her hand up and continued to read. The smile left her face. "They're giving him a medical discharge."

"What happened? Was he hurt?"

She shook her head. "No. He says it's routine. Something called an 'R and R.'"

"What's that?"

"The army's way of saying rest and relaxation."

She folded the letter carefully and put it back in the envelope. "Why would they discharge him if it's just rest he needs? Wouldn't they just give him leave?"

"What does it matter, Mom? He's coming home."

She hesitated, then nodded and tucked the letter in her pocket.

My father came home from Vietnam just before noon on a cool, sunny Saturday in May. My mother spent most of the morning dressing and undressing. Every dress she tried on wasn't right. "I wore this the day he left, didn't I, Tess?"

"What does it matter what you wear?" I said. "Papa won't care."

But the dress was already off and another one was

being thrown over her head. My mother did things like that when she was nervous. She tried to hide it from me, but the other day I'd overheard her tell Mrs. Olney she hoped she'd be able to handle things.

I spent most of the morning in my room, thinking about what my mother had said about war doing strange things to people, hoping she was right about my father being more aware of the important things in life. Us.

Clio called to ask me if I wanted to go to the movies. "I got my father to play you-know-what before the matinee starts. One more chance to see *To Kill a Mocking—*"

"For crying out loud, Clio, didn't I tell you my father is coming home today?"

"Sorry. I thought that was next week. Maybe I can get my father to show it again tomorrow—"

"Tess," my mother called, her heels clicking across the hall floor, "come quickly. Our ride is here."

"I've got to go. The taxi is here."

"The taxi? Did your mother's car break down?"

"She's too nervous to drive."

"She could have asked my father. Or my mother."

"Thanks, Clio. I'll call you."

"Tess." My mother's voice rolled down the hall. "Come on. Now."

"Say hi to your father, Tess. See you tomorrow."

I smoothed my dress, checked myself over in the mirror, and headed to the cab.

My mother and I hardly talked all the way to the airport, but as we drove through the gate and into the terminal, my mother said something about how we should be patient with my father, that sometimes when somebody has been through a traumatic event, it takes a while for them to settle in.

I put my arm around her. "Don't worry. Things will be fine. He just needs some rest, and we can make sure he gets it, right?"

She nodded, but said nothing.

The terminal was dotted with people, some peering out the window, some pacing, all visibly anxious, waiting for the same plane my father was on. When it finally landed on the runway and taxied into the arrival area, my mother took my hand, squeezed it hard, and put it to her chest. I could feel her heart pounding.

"Oh, Tess," she said.

We stood at the doorway and waited. It took a while for passengers to come down the protective walkway. Once they did, names were called out like echoes in a tunnel. "Bill." "Ken, over here." "Liam, thank God." "David."

My mother squeezed my hand harder. "I think I see him." She dropped my hand and took a few steps. "Daniel?" she said, more like a question.

At first I thought my mother had made a mistake. He looked so different, so thin, so old. Shrunken almost. And he walked as though he were walking underwater.

"Nola," I heard him say, reaching for her hand.

I ran over to where they stood.

He turned, his eyes glazed. "Tess," he said, putting his hand on my cheek. He stood as still and pale as a marble statue—only his eyes moved, first toward my mother, then at me. Then rocking back and forth, nodding, he said slowly and softly, "It's good to be home."

Tears spilled down my mother's cheeks, but she was smiling. "Daniel," she said, kissing his cheek. "It's so good to have you back."

I wrapped my arms around him and put my head into the hollow of his shoulder, feeling the warmth of his breath, his hand ruffling my hair. "Welcome home, Papa," I whispered.

"My girls," he murmured. "My girls."

Chapter Two

All afternoon and into early evening my mother and I fussed over my father. I helped him put on his old, caved-in slippers. My mother played his Bach. We served him dinner in the dining room—his favorites, roast rack of lamb with potatoes and onions, creamed spinach, stuffed tomatoes. He hardly ate. "I'm sorry," he said after a few mouthfuls. "I guess the day itself filled me."

My mother got up and went over to him. "There's nothing to be sorry about," she said, taking his plate away.

He nodded and slipped his arm around her waist. "It was delicious."

I always believed only people in the movies cried happy tears, not real people, but I felt like doing just that. I wanted to put my arms around my parents and cover them with kisses, I was so happy seeing them like that, but all I did was begin to clear the table. "You stay here, Mom. I'll do this, then I'll bring dessert." I looked over at my father. "It's custard pie. Do you want just a little?"

He nodded and held up his hand, his thumb and forefinger almost together. "This much."

Just before the kitchen door swung closed behind me, I heard my mother ask my father if there was anything wrong.

I held the door open with my foot.

"Just tired."

"Why don't you go to bed," my mother said. "It's been a long day."

"I don't want to disappoint Tess—"

"You won't disappoint me, Papa," I called back. "When I'm finished, I'll come up to say good night." I let the door close behind me and stood in the kitchen, the dishes cold in my hand, telling myself nothing could disappoint me tonight.

From the kitchen, I heard my father thank my mother and tell her again how good it was to be home. Heard them climb the stairs to their bedroom. Heard the door close behind them.

I stuffed the dishes into our ancient dishwasher, left the pots in the sink, and went out on the back porch. The moon was full, and the sky was a wash of blue velvet filled with millions of stars. I thought about what my mother had said about my father coming home a changed man. She was right. He'd never looked at us the way he had at the airport. Never called us "my girls." And he'd almost cried. Things would be different now. All he needed was some rest. I wanted to celebrate this night.

Trying to remember the words to an old song my father's sister, Treena, used to sing, I began to hum. I took my shoes off and whirled around and around on the damp, cool grass, leaping over the buds beginning in my mother's flower beds. I waltzed under the willow tree, feeling its silky leaves brushing across my face, feeling sure I could fly if I wanted to. I lifted my arms to the sky and sang.

> *"Pack up all your cares and woes,*
> *here I go, singing low*
> *Bye, bye, blackbird—"*

"Tess? Is that you?"

My mother's silhouette was outlined against the porch light.

"I'm over here. Sorry I didn't finish up in the kitchen, but I'm celebrating."

"Forget about the kitchen," she said, making her way toward me, pushing the willow branches aside. "Your father's asleep. He got into bed, closed his eyes, and out he went." She put her arm around me. "Will you look at that moon. My mother always said things went crazy when the moon was full."

"Not tonight," I said.

"Tess," she said, her voice taking on a serious tone, "let's take it slow."

"What do you mean?"

"Your father. Let him go at his own pace for a little while."

"Stop worrying. He's going to be fine."

She put her arm around my shoulders. "But it's going to take time, so let's not rush him. Agreed?"

"Agreed."

"And may I ask what you're doing without your shoes on?" she said, looking down at my feet, visible in the moon's bright light. "It's not summer yet."

"It will be soon."

She nodded, hesitated for a moment, then said, "You're right. Absolutely right." She kicked off her shoes. "What was that you were singing when I came out?"

I hummed and then sang, "Pack up all my cares and woes . . ."

And she answered, "Here we go, singing so . . ."

Then the two of us held hands and swung each other under the willow tree, singing at the tops of our lungs. But when we got to the part, "Won't somebody shine the light, I'll be coming home late tonight," we stopped dancing because the air was broken by a cry, like that of a wounded animal.

We stood, frozen, the willow branches washing over our faces.

"Did the Allens get a dog?" my mother asked.

"No."

Again it sounded, this time like a coyote baying at the full moon.

Without saying a word, we ran across the lawn and into the house, up the stairs, and into my parents' bedroom. The moon's light reached across the bed, and I could see that my father was asleep.

My mother went over to him. "Daniel, are you all right?"

He didn't answer. She put her head close to his for a

minute, then kissed him. "Good night," she whispered, tucking the blankets around him. "Sleep well."

We slipped out of the room and into the hall. "I wonder what that sound was." She shrugged. "Maybe some poor animal got hit by a car. They drive so fast trying to get to the parkway."

She shut the door behind her. "Better get to bed, Tess. Aren't you and Clio meeting Grace Olney at eight tomorrow morning?"

"I'm going to call her and tell her I can't make it. I don't want to go."

"You should have thought of that before. She can't manage twenty seven-year-olds by herself. Besides, it's payback time."

"Why does she have this ridiculous breakfast picnic every year? The kids don't care. All they care about is that it's the last Brownie meeting of the year."

"A promise is a promise." She pushed her shoulder against mine and smiled. "Besides, I seem to remember a seven-year-old who couldn't wait for this ridiculous breakfast. Who got dressed in her uniform at five in the morning."

"But this is different. If I knew Papa was coming home, I wouldn't have promised her."

"Papa won't go anywhere. He'll probably sleep till noon, and you'll be back by then." She kissed me quickly. "I'm going down to put out the lights. See you in the morning."

It was hard to fall asleep, so much had happened this day. I relished the weight of the quilt on my body, the warmth of my bed underneath me. My father down the hall asleep. I felt so safe. A cool breeze blew across my face, my eyes, until it was hard to keep them open.

It was still dark when I woke to the sound of somebody stirring outside my door. I lay there listening to the footsteps making their way downstairs, waiting for the creak of the last three steps. Wrapping myself in my quilt, I headed down the stairs. There wasn't much light—the night-lights my mother always burned weren't on. She feels safer with my father home, I thought.

The glow of a cigarette glared out from my father's office. "Papa?"

No answer.

I reached out and lit the small lamp outside my father's office door. Some of its light leaked into the room, and in the shadows I saw him, sitting at his desk, smoking. Wisps of smoke curled around his head.

"Papa?"

"Who's that?"

"Me. Tess."

"Oh." Just, oh.

"Can't you sleep?"

A deep sigh, the glow from the cigarette brightening. "You go back to bed. I'll be fine."

"I'll make you some cocoa."

Even in the dim light I saw him shake his head. "Go up now, Tess. I'm just . . . just not ready to sleep yet."

Without knowing where it came from, something told me he wanted to be alone, that it wouldn't be right for me to say anything.

In the distance the sound of a train whistle blew through the house like a cold wind. "Good night, Papa," I said, and pulling my quilt tightly around me, I started back to my room.

Chapter Three

"Yesterday was horror day at the movies." It was Clio on the other end of the phone. No Hi or Hello, or How's your father? "The projectionist changed the program," she said. "Nothing but Frankenstein and Dracula. Everybody loved it. Especially Henry S." She laughed. "He said to tell you hi. Are you there, Tess?"

"Is that all you can ever talk about?"

"Since when isn't it all you ever talk about?" And then, "Oh, Tess, I'm sorry. How's your father?"

"Fine."

"Really?"

"Yes. Really."

"You want my father to pick you up? Mrs. Olney said to be at the park entrance at eight."

"Thanks. Bye."

I hauled myself out of bed and went down the hall to the bathroom, first glancing into my parents' room. My father was still asleep.

I showered and dressed quickly, and when I got

down to the kitchen, my mother had fixed eggs for me. She seldom cooked breakfast anymore. We usually set the table the night before, put the box of cereal out with some bananas, and that was it. She'd go off to the clinic, me to school.

"You feel guilty because you're forcing me to go this morning, don't you?"

"That's right. Guilty as charged." She poured me a glass of milk. "I'll drop you off at the park," she said, "then I'll go downtown to pick up the newspapers."

"Clio called. Mr. Holden is driving."

"When did she call?"

"Just a little while ago."

"Oh," she said, shaking her head, "I shut off the bell on our phone. I wanted your father to sleep in."

"He was up last night. He was smoking. He never did that before."

"I know." She came over and hugged me. "He's going to be okay. Things take time. Don't worry." She kissed the top of my head. "Say hi to Clio's dad and thank him for me. I'm going back to bed."

In the car, all Clio talked about was what a great time she'd had the day before. How Francis DeVine got up in front of the screen and imitated Frankenstein's monster. How Billy Palmer took her good coat, swung it around his shoulders like a cape, and made like Dracula. "It was hysterical."

"It's not hi-sterical," I said, annoyed at her for not asking about my father. "It's *hiss*-terical."

"Hi . . . he . . . hiss," she said. "It was infinitesimally funny."

"I think you mean infinitely funny."

I was being mean and I knew it. Usually I laughed when Clio used the wrong word.

"Infinitesimal is just the opposite of infinite," I said.

"Who are you, the walking dictionary?"

"Clio," her father said, an unfamiliar edge to his voice. Then gentler, "Tess, how's your father?"

"He's fine. Tired, but fine."

"Soon as he's settled in, we'd like you all to come for dinner. Tell your mom Mrs. Holden will call within the next week or so."

"I will," I said. Then I reached over to Clio and mumbled, "I'm sorry."

She gave me one of her oh-that's-okay looks. "You know me, the original Mrs. Blooper."

Mr. Holden pulled up to the entrance of the park, where clusters of Brownies and their parents were waiting for Mrs. Olney. "This is the last place I want to be today," I said. "The absolute last."

"It's only for a couple of hours," Clio said, getting out of the car. She called back to her father to pick us up at noon.

As soon as Mrs. Olney arrived the parents fled like cockroaches when the lights go on. "Okay, ladies," Mrs. Olney called out to Clio and me, "the fun begins."

Clio and I grilled sausage links while Mrs. Olney made pancakes, and when the last pancake was gone, Clio started a game of kickball. I stayed back to help Mrs. Olney pack up.

"I didn't want to tell your mother until everything was settled," she said, dousing the coals with water, "but things are in place now." She turned and smiled at me. "The hospital staff is having a welcome home party for your father. Everybody who was at his going-away party wants to be there to welcome him back."

I thought about that going-away party. It was supposed to have been a small party, but it got so big, the crowd spilled out from the cafeteria to the back lawn. Even though my mother was upset about my father going off, she stood at the cafeteria's entrance welcoming each guest, thanking each one for coming, making sure they found their way out to where the food was set up. Mrs. Gargan, the lady who ran the cafeteria, kept urging my mother to mingle. "I'll take care of the door, Mrs. Ramsey," she said. "Your place is with the guest of honor."

I trailed after my father, listening to mothers thank him for saving the babies they held in their arms, watching him comfort a tearful woman, hearing somebody say my father's hands were blessed by God Himself.

Over and over I heard people tell my father to take care of himself, not to take any foolish chances in Vietnam, and I heard my father tell them not to worry, promising he'd come back. He talked and smiled more than he ever did at home. I was jealous. Angry.

After the party, when I was going to bed, my mother and I talked about it. "Sometimes," she said, trying to make me feel better, "people act differently with people they're not emotionally involved with."

"But he is emotionally involved with those people."

She shook her head. "Tess," she said, "your father is

a fine surgeon and a good man, and he cares about what he does, but if he let his emotions take over every time he operated on somebody's child, he couldn't do what he does. You've heard him calm parents who are half crazy with worry, pacify frightened children. What good would it do anybody if he did otherwise?

"Besides, Tess, he's never been one to let his emotions surface." She pulled my quilt under my chin and kissed me good night. "But he loves us. Right?"

I nodded. "But sometimes I wish he were more like you."

"You couldn't stand it," she said, laughing. "We're good for one another just the way we are, your father and me. Can you picture two just-alike people living together? Never works." She reached out and put out my bedside lamp. "Now get some sleep."

It took me a long while to get to sleep that night, and now the same thought came to me: My father was home, but just as he used to bring the hospital home with him, had he brought Vietnam home, too?

The welcome home party didn't happen for three weeks. Even then my mother was dubious about its taking place. My father had had lots of sleepless nights and when that happened, he went down to his office and smoked for hours. It was funny, him smoking. He used to tell people how bad it was to take a foreign matter into your system. Sometimes my mother would sit with him for a while. I knew what she wanted him to do—talk. Talk about why he couldn't sleep. Why he was smoking so much. Why he seemed to want my mother or me around him, but wouldn't let us get really close to him.

My mother told Dr. and Mrs. Olney that the party couldn't be a surprise, that it would be entirely my father's decision. They suggested she discuss it with him.

She did, telling him it was his choice. Whatever he wanted to do. There was plenty of time. At first he said no, a party wasn't necessary. He was back and that was enough. And then, one sleepless night, he agreed to go. "Maybe I should. But small, Nola, no fuss. Just a small gathering."

My father gave my mother a list of twelve or so staff members. The gathering was set for Saturday, June third.

The Olneys agreed. No more than fifteen or so. No fuss.

But something went terribly wrong. First of all it was ninety degrees and muggy. My father said something about feeling like he was back "over there." Until it was time to leave, he sat on the porch, smoking. My mother kept telling him it was all right to change his mind. He didn't.

Driving to the hospital, my mother at the wheel, my father in the passenger seat, we never stopped talking. About nothing.

—Do you mind if I smoke?

—No, we don't mind.

—Things haven't changed much around here, have they?

—No, they haven't.

—Except for Snouder's Drugstore. What did they do to that place?

—The Historical Society redid it.

—Oh.

The gathering was to be held in my father's old office suite at the hospital. Twelve people, fifteen at most. But when we got to the grounds of the hospital, the high school band was set up on the lawn.

"What's this?" my father said.

"I have no idea."

Behind the band there looked to be a thousand people. Waving. Cheering. Balloons. Banners.

WELCOME HOME, DR. RAMSEY . . . MILWAUKEE CHILDREN'S HOSPITAL IS GRATEFUL TO HAVE YOU BACK.

I thought it was great. All for my father. "Papa," I said, "the whole town is here."

He looked pale and tired.

"Daniel," my mother said, "you don't have to—"

Maybe he was embarrassed not to, maybe he didn't want to disappoint everybody, but he got out of the car. I jumped out and stood beside him. He held on to my arm.

"Let's wait for your mother," he said, watching her pull into his old parking spot.

"The fools," my mother said when she joined us, taking my father's other arm. "They are doing exactly what I told them not to do."

Dr. and Mrs. Olney hurried across the lawn. "Nola," Dr. Olney said, "we had no idea—"

"Believe me," Mrs. Olney said, "we did what you said. Somebody in admissions—"

The band began to play Colonel Bogey's march, the crowd clapping in time. Awkwardly, as Colonel Bogey played, we made our way to where everybody waited, and all I could think of was me playing the waltz in Mrs. Otis's gym class.

Chapter Four

Unlike his going-away party when he mingled with everybody, my father never let my mother out of his sight this time. He was like a lost ship keeping the light of the harbor in view. I trailed behind like the dinghy.

People tried to make small talk. A few people asked him about where he'd been, but everybody asked him when he was coming back to the hospital. He shrugged and said things like, "We'll see," or, "In time."

It was my mother who, after a very short time, announced that we would be leaving. A groan went through the crowd, but when my father waved his good-bye and we started toward the car, the band started up again. "Dixie," they played, of all things.

I woke to voices coming from my parents' room. I slipped out of bed and went down the hall.

"I can't stay here," my father said.

"What are you talking about?"

"Being there today, I know I can't go back."

"Nobody expects you to go back right away."

"You don't understand."

"I'm trying. Help me."

"Nola, I need to be in a place where people won't pressure me. Ask me to do things I can't do anymore."

"What do you mean?"

"Operate."

"You don't have to. You have other choices."

"Do I?"

"See somebody. Talk about it."

"I have."

"Over there? What did they know about you? See somebody here. See Stan Guterson or Dave Olney."

"I can't."

"Why?"

"They weren't there. Nobody was."

"Daniel, listen to—"

"No, you listen to me. Do you remember the offer I had before I went to Vietnam? The one in Savannah with a research lab?"

"You didn't want that."

"Then. But I've been giving it a lot of thought. I called them, and they're still open to my coming. There'll be no pressure."

After a long pause I heard my father say, "I'm going to try it. I've got to."

"Don't make decisions you'll regret. Give yourself time."

"I won't live the length of time it will take."

"Talk like that is foolish."

My mother says that a lot—talk is foolish—then she

always adds, "it's the walk that counts." But this time, all she said was, "Daniel, let me help you. Let me in. Please." Her voice was gentle, almost pleading.

I went back to my room and waited until I heard the door to my parents' room close and heard my mother's footsteps going down the stairs. I followed.

She was in my father's office, standing by the window.

"Mom?"

She held her arm out, motioning for me to come to her.

Putting her arm around my shoulders, she said, "You heard, didn't you?"

I nodded.

"I don't know, Tess. I'm so confused, I don't know what to do. I'm going to call Dave Olney tomorrow when I get to the clinic. I don't know what he can do, but I've got to talk to somebody."

"What about us?"

"What do you mean, us?"

"What are we going to do?"

"Oh, my God, you think he wants to leave us, don't you?"

I nodded.

She sighed a heavy, deep sigh. "He would never do that. He wants us to go with him."

She hugged me to her. "And all I can think of is how do I tell your aunt Helen. She's due in eight weeks. She's miscarried four times and she really believes that I'm the one who's gotten her this far. How do I tell her I won't be here for her?"

* * *

My mother did talk to Dr. Olney. He told her there was really no way she could force my father to stay in Milwaukee, no more than she could have prevented his going to Vietnam. He said that many of his own patients thought the way my father did, that another place was the answer—"the old geographic cure," he'd called it. "I don't subscribe to the theory, but amazingly enough, a few of them succeed. Who's to say? Time to let go, Nola. None of us is omnipotent."

From the day it was decided we would go to Savannah, my father seemed more relaxed. He packed up some of his books, hired somebody to rent out the house, saw to it that the car was checked over, and kept reassuring my mother and me that this was the thing to do. But he still had trouble sleeping and would sit in his office smoking for what seemed like hours almost every night.

I hated the idea of moving. I'd always lived in Milwaukee and even though I sometimes hated the long, cold winters, I loved the city. But I kept thinking about what Dr. Olney had said about geographical changes—the ones that worked. Maybe we'd get lucky and be one of those geographical miracles.

Clio cried when I told her I was leaving. She promised that she'd come to visit, that we would always be best friends, and made me promise I'd be back.

She gave me a travel journal, telling me to write down everything about the trip. "Open it," she said. "Look what I wrote."

> For Tessa, my absolved (just kidding) ABSOLUTE best friend,
> Love from Clio.

"You sure you're coming back?" she asked for the hundredth time.

I wasn't sure of anything, certainly not of coming back, but I promised for the hundredth time that I would.

The night before we were to leave, my aunt Helen had strong contractions and the baby's heartbeat was irregular. The doctors thought she would deliver prematurely, but things stabilized by morning. Even so, Helen was sure the baby would come any time and made my mother promise not to leave until she delivered.

"It could be weeks," my father said.

"Or days," my mother said. "What would a few days matter?"

But days turned into a week, and as each day passed, my father became more irritable, more anxious to leave. So we did. Without my mother.

"We'll be fine, Nola," my father said, heading to the garage with things to be packed in the car. "We'll be in Savannah by the first of the week. Right, Tess?"

He was out the door before I could answer.

My mother busied herself around the kitchen, as though she didn't know what else to do with herself. "Tess," she said, putting a glass of juice in front of me, "as soon as Helen delivers, I'll be on the next plane." She ran her fingers through her hair. "God, I feel torn."

"I wish we weren't going," I said. "I wish things could get better right here."

"Then why did you agree to go without me?"

I sighed. "Maybe it will be good for Papa."

"That's not your job, to make it good for Papa. Or for me. You know you can change your mind."

I shook my head. "You'll be coming soon. And he shouldn't go by himself."

"Oh, Tessa," she said, reaching into her skirt pocket. "Here," she said, handing me a small spiral notebook. "I've put down some telephone numbers. There's the clinic—"

"I know that number."

"It's the beeper. Just in case you need me and I'm out of the office."

"What do you think is going to happen?"

"Nothing. It just makes me feel better. And remember, you call me every night. You hear? And if I happen to be out, if Helen's baby comes, leave a message and a number where you are."

She got up and poured herself a cup of coffee. "Treena's number is there, too."

"Why?"

"Taloosa is practically on the way. Maybe you can give her a call."

I heard the start of the car's motor, heard the pebbles crunch under its wheels as my father backed it out of the garage.

"He's ready," my mother said.

She came over and stood behind me and put her arms around me. "I hope that baby comes soon."

"So do I."

"Did I tell you what she's going to name it?"

I shook my head.

"If it's a girl, Nola. And if it's a boy, Nolan. Poor little thing." She hugged me hard. "Oh, Tess, " she whispered, "my harvester, my reaper. Do you realize this is the first time we've been apart? Call me. Every night. Promise?"

I nodded, afraid to trust my voice.

On the driveway, my mother said a long good-bye to my father, and then we were ready to go. I sat where my mother should have been. My mother stood on the path, trying hard not to cry.

"Daniel, I told Tess she's to call every night."

"I know."

She came over, put her head in the window, and kissed me. "I'll miss you."

Then she ran around to the driver's side. "I'll miss you, too." She reached in and kissed him.

"It's just for a short while."

"I know," she said, backing away from the car. "Better get started."

My father shifted into reverse and headed down the driveway.

"Drive carefully," my mother called out. "I love you, Daniel. I love you, Tess. I'll see you as soon as—"

But the engine drowned out her words.

Chapter Five

We drove most of the morning, not talking very much. When we did, it was about the scenery. About two o'clock we pulled into one of those drive-in restaurants, the ones you see in old movies, where all the kids hang out. But this one was empty except for a school bus with no kids, just the lady bus driver hunched over a newspaper, a paper coffee cup in her hand.

A voice boomed over the loudspeaker, asking my father what he wanted to order. When my father reached out for the microphone, the voice told him not to touch it, just to speak up so she could hear.

He looked over at me. "Hamburgers and Cokes?"

"Fries, too."

He used to say fries and burgers were not fit for human consumption. "Garbage," he used to say. But now, he even asked if I wanted cheese on the burger.

Lighting another cigarette, he said he felt tired and that as soon as he saw a decent motel, we'd stop for the day.

Over the loudspeaker the voice said, "That'll be three dollars and twenty cents. Pay the server."

The server stood next to the car, a tray propped next to her shoulder, chewing gum, waiting to be paid. As my father handed her the money, she blew the biggest bubble I ever saw. It popped and the gum went all over her face. I laughed but stopped when I looked over at him. His face was as white as the bag she handed him, his lips drained of color.

"Here's your change," the girl said.

He shook his head. "Keep it."

He handed me the bag and, staring straight ahead, took deep breaths, holding them in, slowly letting them out. He tried to take a cigarette out of the pack, but his hands shook so badly, he couldn't.

"What is it, Papa? What's the matter?"

"Nothing," he said, again trying to take a cigarette from the pack. "Get this for me, will you?"

I did. I even helped him light it. He drew on it slowly and after a long while, the shaking stopped and his color came back.

"What did she do that upset you so much?"

"What did who do?"

"The waitress."

"Nothing. I'm all right."

Reaching over I took the cigarette out of his hand and gave him his hamburger. "You need to eat. You haven't had anything since breakfast, and you didn't eat much then."

"Little Nola," he said, taking a few small bites of the burger, then wrapping it up. "I'm not hungry. Besides, we'd better get on the road again. We don't want to be driving in the dark."

"You used to like to drive at night. You always said the roads were less crowded, and seeing the headlights made it easier."

"Did I?"

"Ask Mom, she'll tell you."

"Well," he said, starting up the motor, "I'd just as soon travel by day when I'm not familiar with the area."

We stopped just before dark at a Hoosier Inn and when we were settled into connecting rooms, my father called in to say he was going down to check out the motel's restaurant. "We'll have an early dinner."

I took out the journal Clio had given me and put in my first entry:

Early evening on June third. . . . We're at the Hoosier Inn. I'm missing home. . . .

I felt restless, didn't feel like writing, so I took a long bath and washed my hair, then picked up the telephone and dialed home. One ring, no answer. Two rings. Maybe she's in the shower. Three rings. Maybe outside. Four rings. Not being able to talk to my mother upset me. For the two years my father was away there was only my mother and me. And now there is only my father and me. An ache began in my chest. "One foot in front of the other," my mother's voice echoed. "When one is melancholy, one needs to move."

I slid out of my robe and into my clothes and went down to the lobby.

"Looking for someone?" the lady behind the desk asked.

"My father."

"Try Trudy's. Most of the customers amble on over there after checking out our restaurant."

My father was at a table by the window. When he saw me standing in the doorway, he came over, an odd look on his face, as though he hadn't expected me. "Tess, yes, Tess, we'll eat now."

After we were seated he asked if I cared if he smoked. Before I could answer, he reached into his pocket, slipped a Camel from the pack, and lit it.

"You never smoked before," I said.

"I know. There are so many things I never did before. . . ." His voice trailed off. He smiled, and for one long minute he seemed to be really there.

And then the waitress came for our order and, as though the smoke from my father's cigarette was a wall between us that sound couldn't break through, we ate our dinner in silence.

Chapter Six

> June fourth—Today was a long day. Papa wanted to make time and so we left the Hoosier Inn right after breakfast, stopped for a fast lunch and, again, just before dark we pulled into the Grand View Motel, where there is no grand view. Where in fact there is no view at all. The manager told me they lost their view when the town built a housing complex for senior citizens across the road. He grinned at me and said that when the time came for him to move on over to the complex, he hoped they'd give him a back room so he could see the view he used to see at the motel.

"Tess," my father called from the other side of the door, "are you ready to get something to eat?"

"I want to get Mom on the phone first."

"Let me know when she's on."

"Okay." And then, "Mom? It's me, Tess."

"Where are you?"

"The Grand View Motel in Indiana."

"How's it going?"

"Wait a sec," I said, making sure the door to my father's room was closed.

When I finished telling her what happened at the drive-in restaurant, she asked if the waitress had said anything to my father.

"No, she just popped the bubble."

"His nerves are on edge. The noise probably startled him. Are things going all right otherwise?"

"I guess. But most of the time it's like he's in another place."

"Remember what I said about giving him time?" she said. "God, I miss you. Papa, too. The house seems like a mortuary."

"Papa wants to speak to you when we're finished."

"Listen, Tess, you be good, and I'll see you before you know it."

> *Still June fourth—had dinner and took a walk around the motel. I'm feeling so lonely. Papa tried to be where his body is but didn't succeed. I miss Clio. She would be hi-sterical talking to the manager of this motel. He looks just like Herman Munster. . . .*

I must have fallen asleep, because it took me a while to realize the voice that woke me was my father's.

"I'm getting out. Do you hear me?" he shouted. "Out of here. This kid is dead. Jesus. Get me out of here—"

I leaped up and ran into his room. He was sitting up in bed, his hands over his ears, his eyes closed, as though he was shutting out something or someone too ugly to look at. "Get out!" he cried. "Get out before they get you, too."

"Papa. Papa." But he didn't hear me.

He cried out again and again. He opened his eyes and looked at me, but I knew he didn't see me, knew he wasn't crying out to me.

Somebody pounded on the door. "Security. What's going on?"

I opened the door.

"You all right?"

I nodded.

"What happened?"

"He had a nightmare."

He went over to my father, whose eyes were closed again. "Look at me," the guard said, waving his hand in front of my father's face. My father didn't open his eyes, but cried out again and again, "I can't help . . . Christ, I can't help . . ."

The guard put his hand on my father's shoulder. "Nobody's going to hurt you. Come on now, open your eyes."

My father held out his hand. "I tried. I always try . . ."

"I don't think you should wake him," I said, lifting the sheet and wiping my father's forehead. "Maybe it's better if he just goes back to sleep."

"Better he gets out of it," the guard said. "Come on,

wake up." He slapped my father's face gently. "Wake up. You'll be okay."

My father was rigid. The guard slapped him a little harder. "Open your eyes. Come on, open them."

Slowly, my father's eyes opened. He looked around, his whole body shaking.

I pulled the blanket around him.

He looked at me. "Where are we?"

"Indiana. At the Grand View Motel."

"What time is it?"

"Three o'clock," the security guard said.

My father held his head in his hands, and rocked back and forth, moaning as though he was in pain. After a while, he reached for his cigarettes.

The guard helped him take one out of the pack and lit it for him. Turning to me, he asked me to watch that my father didn't flick the ash around. "I'm going down to rustle him up a little brandy, see if that will settle him down."

My father looked at me and said he was sorry he'd frightened me. "I'm fine now. You go on back to bed."

"Don't leave," the guard said. "You stay put till I get back."

I took Papa's free hand in mine, rubbing it the way my mother did whenever I needed comfort. "It's all right," I said. "You just had a bad dream." I sat on the edge of the bed, hoping he'd tell me about it, but all he did was draw more deeply on his cigarette.

Sitting there I felt as if I were back at the Monarch Theater with Clio, watching our favorite movie. Only this time it wasn't Atticus Finch I thought of. It was Boo

Radley, the character who was afraid to leave the house, who peered out from behind closed curtains. Who was afraid to speak to anybody, even little children.

When the security guard came back, I kissed my father good night, went back to my room, and almost immediately, miraculously, fell asleep. I didn't wake up until the sun streamed across my face.

I lay there for a while, looking at the water-stained wallpaper, the bare lightbulb hanging from the ceiling, the thin, frayed quilt covering the bed, wishing I were back in my room, suddenly afraid to be alone with my father.

I dialed home, but there was no answer.

I forced myself to shower and dress, and when I heard my father moving around in the next room, I knew what I had to do.

Chapter Seven

It seemed strange to be going to Treena's. In all the time I'd lived, I'd never seen my aunt's home. She usually visited us during holidays from Cor Maria, the convent school where she taught. She'd spend two nights with us, then she'd go to the Bedford Inn. She didn't believe two families should spend more than a weekend under one roof.

When I dialed her number, I wondered if she'd want us out in two days. Would she want us at all? But when we spoke, I could feel her smiling through the telephone. "Of course," she said. "What a wonderful surprise."

When she asked to speak to my father, I thought he would be angry with me because I hadn't told him I was going to call her. But he wasn't. He seemed relieved, glad almost.

In the car he even talked a little about how Treena was more like a mother to him than a sister. She was really his half sister. After Treena's mother died, my grandfather married my father's mother. Treena was nine.

Lighting up another cigarette, my father told me how his mother was sick most of the time. "I can remember your aunt Treena getting up early on Sunday morning, getting us ready for church, then coming home to cook Sunday dinner."

"What was the matter with your mother?"

He shrugged. "Nerves. Whatever. It was always something."

"How old was Treena when you were born?"

"Eleven."

My mother had pictures of my father as a baby, most of them with Treena. She looked so much older than eleven, maybe because she was so tall. That was the only thing my father and Treena had in common, their height. My father was so handsome, he could be Gregory Peck's understudy. Treena wasn't pretty at all.

She wasn't fat, but large-boned, as my mother always said. I once asked her how far she could stretch her fingers on the piano keyboard. She asked me where she should start. I told her at middle C. I watched as her pinkie inched up all the way to "F." Eleven notes. Even now I can only reach to "D."

My father lit another cigarette.

"She's not going to like your smoking," I said, surprised at myself for saying that.

He looked over at me, a queer expression on his face. "I don't like it myself," he said.

"Then why do you do it?"

He didn't answer, just put the cigarette out and kept driving.

We drove along winding roads, past fields of fruit

trees, past empty farm stands, past houses standing alone in treeless spaces. My mother always wondered how Treena, who loved opera and theater, could live in a place like Taloosa.

I remember my father telling my mother it was the first time in her life she could choose for herself. And she chose Taloosa.

"This is it," my father said, turning into a dirt driveway that sloped down sharply, then wound around and around until we were finally there, at Treena's. The small, gray house with purple shutters sat in the center of a clearing, woods surrounding it.

Treena was standing on the front porch, wearing worn overalls and muddy boots. As soon as the car stopped, she clumped down the stairs. "Tessa," she called, "come and give me a hug."

"Oh," she said, squeezing me to her, "I think I've died and gone to my Creator." Cupping my chin, she studied my face. Her palms smelled like rich soil. "You're as pretty as your mother," she said, kissing my forehead.

And then, looking toward my father, her eyes misted over. "Danny," she whispered.

She was the only one who called my father Danny.

My father got out of the car. "Danny," she said, releasing her hold on me, "what have they done to you?"

Gathering him to her, she hugged him, and he began to cry. Openly, without shame. I heard him say he didn't think he could go on to Savannah. He was not himself. He hadn't been for so long, he wondered if he would ever be again. He said it wasn't good for me to be alone with him. And finally, he said, "Can we stay awhile?"

And as though he were a child, Treena ruffled his hair, held his face in her hands, and said, "Danny, you can stay forever."

Chapter Eight

"It's good to have you here," Treena said as she placed scrambled eggs before me. "And at the right time."

She poured herself coffee and sat across from me. "I've only got three days left at school and then I'm free for the rest of the summer, except for some tutoring." She took a long drink, then put her coffee cup down and reached over and put her hand on mine. "Tell me, Tess, how long has your father been like this?"

"Ever since he came home."

"Has he seen a doctor? A psychiatrist?"

"No. He told my mother he'd see one when we got to Savannah."

"That's nonsense. He'll see somebody here." She smiled at me. "That I can promise you." She got up and piled eggs and toast on a plate, poured a glass of orange juice, fixed a mug of coffee with cream, and placed everything on a tray. "Tell you what. You take this on up to your father, then get dressed. You're coming to school with me."

"But what about Papa?"

"What about him?"

"He'll be alone."

"So?"

"He smokes so much. What if he drops—"

"I've already told him he can't smoke in the house. The porch or the yard, but not the house." She pushed the tray toward me. "He still listens to me."

"But—"

"No buts. You get dressed now. I have to be there by eight."

It had rained a hard summer rain the night before, and the air smelled of grass and woods. Leaving Treena at her classroom, I made my way across the lawn and stopped by a swimming pool barely visible behind the purple wisteria. Wisteria was everywhere, climbing up brick walls, hanging over trellises, porches.

Just beyond the pool, the lawn sloped down sharply and I had the urge to roll down it. I looked around to make sure I was alone, gathered my skirt close, lay down, and pushed off. I rolled and bounced down the embankment, and when I reached the bottom I was so dizzy, I could barely stand. When my head stopped spinning, I crossed a small bridge and made my way up a hill until I was standing in front of a small chapel, the bell in its tower ringing in the hour.

In the distance I heard a voice call, "Rapunzel, Rapunzel, let down your hair." A girl ran toward me, her yellow dress billowing around her like a parachute.

"Just kidding," she said, smiling, catching her

breath. "Rapunzel's not really up there, but somebody is. I heard them laughing one morning." She looked up at the tower. "I'm going to catch them one of these days." And then, turning to me, she said, "You're new here, aren't you?"

I nodded.

"Great," she said. "I finally found somebody in Taloosa who is newer than I am."

"What do you mean?"

"We've been here for over a year, and everybody still calls us the new people. We're always the new people." She shrugged. "My mother and I move around a lot. How about you?"

Without waiting for an answer, and as though she had known me forever, she slipped her arm into mine. "Come on," she said, gently pulling me along with her, "I've got to sign in at the office. I've got a makeup test fourth period with Mrs. Cooper, also known as Attila the Hun."

I stopped and pulled my arm away. "She's my aunt."

She shrugged. "Sorry, but everybody calls her that. She knows we do." She slipped her arm through mine again. "She's okay. Really. She's everybody's favorite, even though she's tough."

She tightened her grip on my arm and started to walk again. "I'll sign in at the office, then I can show you around. Okay?"

"I don't think so."

"Come on," she said. "I'm one of Mrs. Cooper's favorites. I think."

"I'm meeting her at noon."

"Fine. But it's only nine, and the test isn't till eleven. I can show you around and maybe you can quiz me later. Okay?"

Hesitating for a minute, I said, "Where shall I meet you?"

"Meditating by the swimming pool, under an oak tree, breathing in the fragrance of the wisteria," she said, swinging the door open. "I'm Selina and I'm always around." But before the door closed, she called back, "Meet you at the tower in fifteen minutes. I'll bring some apples."

I watched through the window of the door until she was out of sight, not understanding why I was suddenly feeling better than I'd felt since leaving home.

Stretched out on the grass, eating apples, the sun warming us, I found myself telling Selina things about my father that I never would have told Clio.

"It was so awful being with him the other night," I said. "It was like he was somewhere else. He screamed at somebody to get out, that the boy was dead, saying over and over how sorry he was. And then when I called my mother, she wasn't there."

"Where was she?"

"With my aunt. She's having a baby and she wants my mother to be there for the delivery."

"Your mother is a doctor?"

"No, my father is. My mother is a nurse."

"So what did you do?"

"I decided to come here. It felt like I was the parent and he was the child. It was awful."

She nodded. "I know. I do it all the time."

"Do what?"

"Feel like I'm my mother's mother."

"What do you mean?"

"Because my father is never coming back. It's not that he's dead, he's just not coming back. Ever."

Handing me another apple, she said, "My mother keeps moving, hoping something good will happen in the next place we go." She took a bite from the apple. "I think she's hoping that one day we'll land where my father is."

"I'm sorry," I said.

"So am I. But that's the way it is." She turned and looked at me. "You're lucky. There's hope for your father. Maybe that's why you're here."

"What do you mean?"

"I don't know exactly." She reached out and picked some grass, then sprinkled it between us. "Do you believe in God?"

I nodded.

"Ever since I came here, I've felt like we're home. I've never felt that way before. We've been here longer than we've ever been anyplace. I sometimes think God put us here for some reason. A good one." She shrugged. "You think I'm crazy, don't you?"

"No."

"Anyway, maybe that's why you're here—so your father will find his way. . . . you, too."

A chill went through me. "Maybe," I said. "Maybe you're right."

She sat up and reached for her books. "Now, how

about quizzing me on Chaucer? Your aunt is crazy for Chaucer."

We finished the apples and I quizzed her on Chaucer until it was time for her test. I walked back to the classroom with her, made plans to meet her and Treena for lunch, then decided to go back up to the tower to read. Selina had given me a book of poems, and as I walked I scanned the pages until I found a poem by Frost: "Two roads diverged in a yellow wood, And sorry I could not travel both . . . "

Then from out of nowhere, a motor roared and somebody yelled, "GET OUT OF THE WAY!"

Chapter Nine

I looked behind me and saw a huge power mower heading toward me.

I raced down a steep hill, so steep I couldn't stop until I was ankle deep in water. Behind me footsteps pounded and somebody yelled, "You okay?"

Shaking all over, I screamed, "What's the matter with you? You could have killed me!"

"Hey, I'm sorry, but the brakes slipped."

I tried to move my feet and couldn't. I panicked and started to cry. "Help me! I'm in quicksand."

His hands reached out to me. "It's just mud," he said. "Calm down. I'll get you out."

I clutched his hands.

My feet wouldn't budge.

"Good thing you ran into the shallow part of the lake. A mile or so down and you would have been over your head instead of your ankles."

"That is not funny."

"Hey, I didn't mean it to be funny."

Tightening my grip on his hands, I tried to raise one foot and then the other. They still didn't move. Finally I wiggled out of my shoes and stepped onto the grass.

"You're okay now," he said, reaching down, pulling my shoes from the muddy water.

Taking a rag from his back pocket, he wiped them off. "These don't look so good," he said, handing me my shoes. "I don't think you're going to be able to wear them again."

Reaching for my shoes, I saw his face clearly for the first time. He was the most beautiful person I'd ever seen—taut, almond-colored skin, eyes as dark as chestnuts, his hair black and curly.

"They're old shoes," I lied.

"Well," he said, "the least I can do is drive you back to school."

"I don't go to school here. I'm visiting my aunt."

"So I'll drive you to your aunt's."

"That's not necessary. I'm meeting her at noon in the cafeteria."

"With no shoes?"

I shrugged. "I like to go barefoot."

He motioned for me to get on the mower. "I'll drive you to the cafeteria. It's a hike from here and kind of rocky."

"Are you old enough to drive?" I asked.

"I'm eighteen." He hoisted himself into the driver's seat, then turned and helped me up. "Don't worry," he said, "as long as the brakes work, I can run this thing with my eyes closed."

"Are you the gardener?"

He shook his head and started the mower. "This was my buddy's summer job, but he's out of commission for a while."

Reaching over to release the brake, he asked me if I minded if he mowed as we went along.

"No."

"So," he said, glancing back to check where he'd mowed, "where are you from?"

"Milwaukee."

"Aaah, where they make the beer. Where in Milwaukee?"

"By the lake."

Turning back again, he said, "Cripes," and then quickly, "excuse my language, but I messed up on that." He shifted gears and headed back.

"So how long will you be here?" he asked, guiding the mower carefully back over the parts he'd missed.

"I'm not sure. My father and I are on our way to Savannah."

"How come?" Without waiting for an answer, he looked over where he'd mowed, smiled, and said, "What do you know? Perfection."

We bounced along, the mower's engine sputtering so loud, I could hardly hear him when he told me his name.

"Hal?"

"With a 'C,'" he shouted back. "Cal. Caleb. What's yours?"

"Tess. Tessa Ramsey."

When we reached the cafeteria, he smiled a wonderful smile, and was off.

"So how did you keep yourself busy?" Treena asked as we headed toward the cafeteria.

"Just walked."

"What happened to your shoes?"

"Oh," I said, looking down at my bare feet, "I must have left them down at the lake."

"How about that?" she said. "And how about this? How would you like to work as a camp counselor for the summer?"

"But what about Savannah?"

"Your father isn't up to that. You let me take care of him."

I turned and hugged Treena, almost lifting her off the ground. Selina might be right, I thought. God just might have sent us to Taloosa.

Chapter Ten

This is a very special journal entry and deserves an uncommon opening: It is early evening on the sixth day of June in the year of our Lord nineteen hundred and sixty-eight, the most extraordinary day and year of my life. Not only did I meet Selina this morning, I met Caleb. He said to call him Cal, but it doesn't seem to fit him. Caleb does. I looked up his name in the dictionary as soon as I got to Treena's this afternoon. At first I was horrified at its meaning. "Dog," the dictionary said, but when I read on, it made perfect sense. "Caleb . . . meaning 'dog' (in Hebrew) with the significance of faithful affection." It went on to say that Caleb was one of two men who survived after the forty-year wandering of the Israelites. How simply beautiful all of that is. How simply beautiful Caleb is.

I don't even know his last name. I know I'll see him again because he's working at the convent where Treena teaches, where I'll be working if my father agrees to stay. I think he will. It's not easy to say no to Treena. Even Sister Catherine, who is the Mother Superior of the convent, couldn't. She gave me the job as counselor without even meeting me. Treena told me I'd be helping with swimming lessons in the morning and arts and crafts in the afternoon. I don't care what I do as long as I get to stay.

We've got to stay. My father is really acting strange. I told him about Helen and my mother not knowing when she was going to deliver. It was almost as though he hadn't heard me, and if he had, he didn't care. Treena said not to be concerned, that sometimes when somebody has experienced what he has, they want to distance themselves from anything unpleasant. . . . I don't want to distance myself from here. Maybe it's selfish, but I feel something good will happen here . . . to me. . . .

"Tess," Treena called, "your father's ready."

"Be right there."

Treena doesn't waste any time. She has my father on an exercise program. He's to walk for at least half an hour a night. "You'll sleep better," she told him.

Last night after we had supper—that's what they call dinner in Taloosa—the three of us walked. Tonight there was just my father and me. We hiked up to the main road and walked down to the edge of the park.

My father finished one cigarette and lit up another.

"I hate for you to do that. I really hate it."

"I need it."

"Treena says you need to talk to somebody."

He sighed a long, deep sigh. "When we're settled."

"Here, you mean?"

"When we get to Savannah."

"Didn't Treena tell you she got me a job at the convent?"

He shook his head.

"Well, she did. And I want to take it. I want to stay here. Please, Papa, at least for the summer. At least till Mom gets here."

"We'll talk about it. Decide what to do."

I've made my decision, I thought. "Papa," I said, surprised at what I was about to say, "I'm staying."

He didn't react. It was as though he was in another place, as though we had floated back in time, back to a summer night in Milwaukee, because when an ice-cream truck rounded the corner, he asked me what kind of ice cream I wanted. And he called me Tissy, a name he hadn't called me since I was five.

And then, before I could answer, he said he was tired and needed to go back. Treena was waiting for us on the porch.

"Nola called," she said to my father. "She wants you to call her. It looks as though Helen is losing the baby."

My father started up the stairs. "Danny," Treena called after him, "didn't you hear me?"

"I'm tired," he said. "Very tired."

Treena turned to me and told me to call my mother, then she started up the stairs after my father. "Give yourself time, Danny. Stay for the summer. Or longer. Whatever you need. Do it for yourself. For Tess. You're not ready to take on a research position."

"I'm not ready to do much of anything, am I?"

"You will be. In time."

"Tess, it's almost seven-thirty," Treena called from the kitchen. "There are fresh blueberries whenever you're ready for breakfast. We've got to leave here in about half an hour."

"I'll be ready," I called back, swinging my legs out of bed.

My hair was a mess. I decided to clip it back. I put some Vaseline on my eyelashes to make them notice-able, and pinched my cheeks for some color.

"Tess, it's ten to eight."

"Be ready in five minutes."

Putting on the lipstick, I heard my mother's voice echoing around the room: "Remember, Tess, a little goes a long way." I leaned close to the mirror and blotted it carefully. Looking at the imprint of my lips on the tis-sue made me think that I'd never really kissed a boy. Francis DeVine once sneaked a kiss in the movies, but then he kissed just about every girl, whether he knew her or not. Some of the girls thought it was fun. I didn't. Kissing a boy is serious, and going around kissing just anybody isn't something I consider fun. . . .

"Tess, I'm going to be late. Hurry."

"I'm coming."

In the kitchen I quickly drank a glass of milk, took some blueberries and a banana, and followed Treena to the car.

We were almost at the convent before I thought of my father. I hadn't even said good-bye. I felt guilty, as though I had abandoned him, but as soon as Treena pulled into the convent gates, the feeling left me and a lightness came over me.

"Meet you at the cafeteria at noon," Treena said.

"At noon," I said, all but flying from the car.

I spent the morning looking for Caleb. Just before noon, I went down to the lake and there, by the shore, were my shoes, placed carefully on a rock.

I thought of a story I had once read, about a girl who lost her shoes at an ice-skating pond. Unknown to her, the most unpopular boy in her school found them, a boy who has loved her but has never had the courage to tell her. He tucked a note in one of her shoes that said, "J'adore tes petits pieds," and left them at her door. Her mother found the note and thought the girl was seeing somebody strange, somebody who loved feet, her daughter's little feet. She forbade the girl to see that somebody. The girl never found out who wrote the note, but every time she wore those shoes she felt that, like Dorothy, they could take her anywhere. Maybe even to Oz.

There wasn't a note in my shoes, nothing that said Caleb was here, nothing that said we'll see each other again. Only my mud-streaked shoes waiting for me.

Chapter Eleven

"Wait up," a voice called.

I turned and watched Selina run toward me, holding her chest. "You walk too fast," she said between breaths.

"Why didn't you just call out?"

"That's what I've been doing. I yelled 'Hey, Tess' a hundred times, but you just kept going." She took a deep breath, then, standing on her tiptoes, she put her finger on the end of her nose, arched her throat, and said, "Well, Miss Ramsey, I have been asked to be kind enough to tell you that your aunt will not be able to meet you for lunch. I'm also to be so kind as to tell you she'll meet you at three o'clock by the gate."

"She doesn't talk like that."

Selina laughed and said, "That was Sister Catherine talking. Your aunt got held up at a meeting." Slipping her arm through mine, she said, "Come on, I'm starved. Let's eat."

"I don't have any money. I was supposed to meet my aunt."

"We can go to Bailey's Luncheonette downtown. I've got enough money for that."

Selina took my hand and swung our arms back and forth as we headed toward the convent gates.

"If I tell you something," she said, "promise you won't tell?"

"About what?"

"I heard your aunt ask Sister Catherine about hiring a groundskeeper for the convent."

"So?"

"She said her brother might 'fit the bill.' Those were her exact words. So the way I figure it, her brother has got to be your father. Right?"

"Right. But he's not a groundskeeper."

"I know. I guess Sister Catherine forgot she had asked me to wait outside her office, and she talks so loud I could hear everything. Honest, I tried not to listen because I felt sorry for your father. It's sad, him being a doctor and not being able to practice."

If Clio had said she felt sorry for my father, it would have bothered me. But, for some reason, hearing it from Selina, I didn't mind.

"He doesn't know a thing about gardening. He'd never agree to that."

"He could learn. At least that's what your aunt said. She said he needs something that's strictly physical. Nothing mental."

"I don't know about that. Physical work, I mean. Since he came home, he has no energy for anything."

"Maybe this will energize him. You want to stay, don't you?"

"Sure. I even told my father I've made up my mind to stay, but I know darn well if he decides to go, I'll go with him."

"Don't be so negative. Maybe he'll surprise you and take the job."

I shook my head. "Never. He barely talks to Treena and me. How is he going to talk to people he doesn't know?"

"Who is he going to talk to mowing grass? The squirrels? The bees? Besides, yesterday we didn't know each other and look at us now."

"That's different."

"No it isn't. Sometimes people talk more to strangers than they talk to their own family. I'll bet you do that, too?"

"Do what?"

"Barely talk to him. Ask him what's bothering him."

And then, as though I'd lost control of my tongue, I told her how angry I was with my father. How I'd waited for him to come home, believing my mother was right, about him changing for the better. "But he hasn't. He's worse. I am so tired of trying to make him talk. And I'm tired of his smoking. Last night he really made me angry. He wouldn't talk to my mother. It's as though he's the only one who's hurting.

"It is so hard having him sitting next to me and not be there. I feel like the girl who comes back to earth for one day and nobody knows she's there. Her mother is making breakfast, but she doesn't hear her own daughter calling to her. Nobody notices her. I want him to notice me."

Selina stopped walking. "At least he's there."

I'd forgotten what she'd told me about her father. "I'm sorry. Really."

She shrugged. "What's that saying? What you don't have you don't miss? It's true."

I didn't answer her because if I did, I would have told her that for me it mattered. I did miss what I didn't have. Instead, I put my arm around her shoulders. "Come on, let's eat. My mother always says when you're hungry, everything looks dismal."

The luncheonette was crowded. We ordered grilled cheese sandwiches and Cokes at the counter, then found an empty booth. As soon as we sat down a boy in the next booth turned, messed up Selina's hair, and said, "Hi, Sel."

"It's got to be Walter," she said, smoothing her hair and rolling her eyes.

"Who's your friend?" he asked, looking at me, a straw dangling from his mouth.

"What?" Selina yelled, putting her hand on the back of her neck.

From the straw, Coke dripped down her back.

She grabbed some napkins and wiped her neck. "Do that one more time and you are dead," she said. "D.E.A.D. Dead."

And then, from out of nowhere, he appeared. Caleb. Wearing a white uniform with red stitching on the hat and pocket that read: ASSISTANT MANAGER.

"Maybe not dead, but out of here," Caleb said, taking the straw from the boy, handing him a rag. "We don't appreciate having Coke dripped all over the booths. Clean it."

Then, turning to us, he said, "Sorry. It won't happen again."

I could barely get my breath. "Hi," I said.

"Hi," he said, again turning to the next booth. "Make sure you get it all."

"Caleb?" I said.

"Hey," he said, turning back to me, studying me for a minute, "I didn't recognize you. You do something different to yourself?"

"My hair."

"I tried to hunt you down yesterday. You forgot your shoes."

"I know."

"Did you get them?"

"My shoes?"

"And the note?"

He *did* leave a note. My heart pounded.

From the back, a voice called his name.

He checked the now empty booth behind us and gave it a quick wipe with the rag. "Be right there," he said, and then to us, "See you."

As soon as he disappeared into the back, Selina leaned over and in a loud whisper said, "When did you meet him?"

"Yesterday. At the convent."

"What did he mean about your shoes and the note?"

She sat motionless, her eyes wide, as I told her what happened the day before.

"I can't believe it. You're in Taloosa one day and he

writes you a note." She leaned closer. "What did the note say? I promise not to tell anybody."

"I don't know."

"What do you mean, you don't know? Caleb Girard writes you a note and you forget what he said?"

"I never saw it. When I went down to the lake, all that was there were my shoes."

She slumped back into the booth. "Is he the most magnificent human being you've ever seen?"

I sighed. "Absolutely."

She leaned toward me again. "He's smart, too. He was appointed to West Point. Can you imagine him in that uniform?" She slumped back again. "To die for."

"How do you know him?"

"He's a senior at Cor Maria. He came from California in his sophomore year. He's never said one word to me, or to any other girl in my class, but every one of us would die to get a note from him. Even a hello. Or a look. Or anything. But he's kind of standoffish."

She reached for a french fry. "If I were Rapunzel," she said, dipping the fry into some ketchup, "I'd want Caleb to be the one who climbed up my hair." She sighed, "Oh, well, if it can't be me, then let it be you."

"You're crazy," I said.

She nodded. "I agree."

I popped the last fry into my mouth. When I thought of the possibility of my father taking the job, of our being able to stay, a feeling of serene happiness washed over me—only to vanish when I thought of the alternative.

Chapter Twelve

June seventh . . . I keep thinking of that story about the boy who found the girl's shoes. How he wrote about her little feet and how he loved them—"J'adore tes petits pieds"—the French sounds so much better—"J'adore, J'adore, J'adore." It makes me wonder what Caleb's note said. Maybe he wrote something like that. Or a poem. No, I don't think he'd write a poem, but then I don't really know him. Maybe he would. Maybe he absolutely loves poetry. Maybe even poems about love. Last January we studied Asian poetry. . . . I loved it . . . the one about love . . .

DEAR LOVE
'TIS LESS THAN I HAVE VOWED
BUT LET ME GATHER IN

AND BRING
ALL LOVE
FROM EARTH AND SEA AND SKY;

THEN
LET US TO ITS EQUALING
THAT LOVE,
WHEN DEATH HAS RAVISHED US,
ENCASE OUR SHROUD.*

It's so beautiful. Sad but beautiful. Only thirty-nine words. ". . . that love, when death has ravished us, encase our shroud" says so much more than the one Mrs. Epstein compared it with . . .

HOW DO I LOVE THEE? LET ME
COUNT THE WAYS.
I LOVE THEE TO THE DEPTH
AND BREADTH . . .
I LOVE THEE TO THE LEVEL OF
EVERY DAY'S . . .
I LOVE THEE FREELY . . . I LOVE
THEE PURELY . . .

then something about loving better after death.

Don't remember the rest. I guess it is beautiful in its own way . . . like Mrs. Epstein said . . . we all absorb poetry in different ways. . . . She always used the

strangest words . . . "absorb" . . . like we
were sponges . . . well, anyway. . . .
    I'm praying Papa takes the job as
groundskeeper. But if he does, they won't
need Caleb? But I don't think Papa can
do everything. . . . Selina said the pool
has to be cleaned every day, and the arts
and crafts rooms, and the mowing. . . .
He's never done anything like that before.
. . . Maybe Caleb can help him. . . .

A long, loud wail came from down the hall. Tossing my journal on the bed, I ran toward Papa's room. Treena was ahead of me, calling, "Danny, Danny, what is it?"

"What do you want from me? I can't do it. Understand?"

Treena reached for his hand.

He slapped her away, then pushed her hard. "Stay away from me. Don't you hear what I'm saying? I can't do it."

He was trembling so hard, the bed shook.

"I'm no miracle worker. I can't fix everything—"

"Tess," Treena said, "go down and get the bottle of brandy. Bring a glass—"

All the way down to the kitchen, I heard my father crying out about the mosquitoes and the heat. And when was it going to end.

"Breathe, goddamnit. Breathe," he kept shouting. "I can't do it—"

Even with the brandy, it took a long time for him to

settle down. I sat on one side of the bed, holding a cool cloth to his head; Treena sat on the other, saying over and over that he needed help.

He shook his head and asked for a cigarette. Treena didn't hesitate; she even lit it for him.

"Danny," she said, "I'm arranging something tomorrow. You've got to see somebody."

His voice unsteady, his hand shaking as he put the cigarette into his mouth, he said, "Not yet. Not now."

"Then when?"

He looked at her with a get-this-into-your-head look, but said nothing.

Treena reached over and put her hand on his. He didn't pull away. "You can't stay cooped up like this. Do you hear? You've got to help yourself."

Still, he said nothing.

"Danny, please. Don't do what you've done since you were a kid. You've got to talk about it. You've got to do something. Now."

He drew deeply on the cigarette.

"That you can do," she said. "Contaminate your body. But get help? That's beyond you." She ran her hand through her hair. "I'm too tired to deal with this now," she said, taking the cigarette from my father and dropping it into the empty brandy glass. "We'll talk about it tomorrow."

She tucked the package of cigarettes into her bathrobe pocket, then turning to me, said, "Tess, go to bed. We'll have to get an early start tomorrow."

But I didn't go to bed. I sat with my father, hoping he'd talk. He didn't, at least not what I wanted him to talk about. He talked about possibly leaving for Savannah in a few days.

"I told you, Papa, I don't want to leave here. You said we'd think about it. Remember?"

"I've got a job waiting."

"I don't care. Treena is right. You're not ready to do anything. You need help."

"I'll get it."

"But not here. Is that what you're saying?" I stood up. "I'm not going. Do you hear? I'm not. I'm afraid—"

"Of what?"

"Of being alone with you. It scares me when you're in one of those dreams. You're not here. You don't even know me. At the motel, you looked right through me. Tonight, too. You pushed me away; Treena, too, so hard, she almost fell. . . ."

"Oh, my God," he said softly.

He looked so pathetic, I could feel myself weakening, could feel the tears coming. I turned and started back to my room.

"Tess, wait—"

I kept walking.

I heard his footsteps behind me, but I didn't stop. I got as far as the door to my bedroom, and he was beside me. Putting his hand on my arm, he said, "I'll ask Treena to arrange something. I'm trying, Tess. . . ."

Some part of me wanted to say something to comfort him, wanted to lean over and kiss him, but all I did was nod and say good night.

"Your mother wants you to call her tonight," Treena

said as she opened the blinds to let the morning sun bathe the bedroom.

"She called?"

"Early this morning. Seems like Helen ran into some trouble."

"She lost the baby?"

"No, but she's got to be flat on her back until she delivers."

"She shouldn't be having a baby. She's too old to deal with it all."

"I beg your pardon. Thirty-nine is little more than a child." She poked her head into the closet and took out a blouse. "By the way, your father asked me to look for a therapist."

She came over and put her arm around me. "It's all going to work out fine. You're going to work at the camp, and I've convinced Sister Catherine your father can handle the groundskeeper job. Now all I have to do is convince him." She squeezed me to her. "Helen will deliver her baby, you and your mother and father will be together again, and all will be right with the world."

Driving to the convent, I thought how wrong everything was right now. I decided when I called my mother I was going to tell her that even if my father refused to take the job at the convent and insisted on going to Savannah, I wasn't going to go. I was going to be honest with her. Tell her I was afraid to be alone with him. Tell her how angry I was with him. And with her, too, for putting Helen before us. But by the time we pulled into the convent gates, I felt guilty about that.

If it weren't for Helen, I might not be here. Helen

and my mother were more like sisters than friends. She was the one who got my mother and father together. They were in nursing school, and my father was Helen's professor. She got my mother to come into his class. "He was so gorgeous," Helen told me, "your mother all but floated to her seat. And from that day on, there was nobody else in her life."

It's hard for me to imagine that. My parents were so different from each other. My father was twelve years older than my mother and serious about everything. My mother was serious when she had to be, but mostly she was fun. Helen said that's what attracted him to my mother. He loved to see in her what wasn't in him.

Is that what attracts people to one another? Seeing something in that person that isn't in you? Is that what attracted me to Caleb? I didn't know him well enough to know if there was a difference between us. But I knew how I felt when I first saw him. Different from any feeling I'd ever had.

It's hard for me to imagine something else Helen told me about my father. She told me that when my mother was pregnant with me the doctors wanted her to abort, because her uterus was small and she had been exposed to German measles in her second month. My mother wouldn't hear of it. Helen said my father was frantic, afraid to lose my mother, afraid of what could happen to me . . .

"TESSA RAMSEY." The sound of Treena's voice startled me. "Come back to the living. We're here."

*From *Arabic and Persian Poems,* compiled and translated by Omar S. Pound. Poet: Al-Abbas ibn al-Ahnaf

Chapter Thirteen

My father still hasn't started therapy, but he did take the job as groundskeeper. "Maybe that's all I need," he told Treena, "to keep busy." Treena didn't push, but she did find a psychiatrist, and she's sure my father will come around. I'm more annoyed with him than she is. Treena tells me to be patient, that he promised he'd get help. But he didn't promise when. I find it hard to be patient, especially in the evening when we walk. He avoids all meaningful conversation. If anything comes up that he doesn't want to talk about, he says he's tired and we head back to Treena's. Then he spends the rest of the night on the porch. Last night when I went out to say good night, I watched him for a while from the doorway. He was smoking, the *smoke drifting around his head like a halo. It hurt to see him like that. It made me feel more alone, as though the cigarette was his only comfort. When my hurt doesn't get resolved, it turns to anger. I felt so angry, I went to bed without saying good night to him.*

Every once in a while I talk to Treena about how I feel. She understands, but tells me to get on with things, to enjoy Selina and what's going on at the convent. To stop focusing on my father so much. When I'm with Selina, I do, and the more we're together, the more I like her. I wish I could say that about Caleb, I mean being together, because we haven't been . . . but I think about him all the time. Is that what love is? Thinking about somebody? Imagining things about that somebody? I've only met him twice and yet I dream about him. The other night I imagined my wedding. In the dream, I was wearing my mother's wedding dress . . . ecru lace, my mother told me, not white. The sleeves were long with lots of tiny satin buttons. I had trouble buttoning them. My mother helped me. In the dream she wasn't her usual happy self. She was frowning and asked me over and over if I was sure about what I was doing. "I am," I said. When the last but-

ton was buttoned, she said, "Remember you're still Tessa Ramsey. Don't ever forget it." That's when I woke up.

I haven't told Selina that I think I love Caleb, because I think she likes him, too. We're working now—we had to get special papers since we're only fifteen and can only work so many hours a day. Three days a week we do arts and crafts with six- and seven-year-olds. It's fun. Then, if we pass the swimming test, the other two mornings we'll be helping out at the pool. If you're a strong swimmer you get to lifeguard, otherwise you just help with the kids. I don't really care what I do, I'm enjoying it all. AND, AND, AND, Selina and I get our first paychecks today and we're going to Bailey's for lunch. We've walked by there a few times, but there's always somebody else behind the counter. Not Caleb. Please God, let him be there and I'll never ask for another thing. I take that back. There's too much going on to keep a promise like that. There's something else I'm praying for. My father definitely needs help at the convent. He seems overwhelmed at times. Please, God, let him ask for help and let it be you-know-who who gets the job.

❖   ❖   ❖

"Tess," Treena called, as she did every morning, "it's getting late."

"Coming," I said, checking my hair for the hundredth time, checking to see that my shorts were long enough. Sister Catherine had a thing about shorts. On Tuesday, she called a meeting of all the counselors—girls, that is. "There will be no exceptions. If I see anybody wearing any shorts other than the type described in the pamphlet you were given, that person will answer to me." No short shorts. They have to be no more than two inches above the knee. And then she issued bathing suits. Clio would say they were Hi-larious. Ugly, is what I say. Black, one-piece, itchy things. Not only are they black and itchy, stitched on the back is PROPERTY OF COR MARIA CONVENT. As though we would be caught dead in them anywhere else.

We had to try them on, too, "For proper fit," as Sister Catherine said, which when translated means, "Nobody is to have a suit that fits or in any way shows any part of the anatomy—from neck to thighs." Selina and I almost fell down laughing when we looked in the mirror. I told Selina that with her blond hair and long legs, she looked like Miss America. The *first* Miss America. She said I looked like Mary Tyler Moore, without breasts, and wearing a bathing suit Aunt Bee had purchased in Mayberry, RFD.

Treena put her head into the bedroom. "Let's go. It's almost eight."

Going through the kitchen, I took some fruit and drank a glass of milk. Then I went out to the car.

My father sat in the front seat in his uniform. It was

so hard to get used to that. My father, who used to wear suits and ties and, when he was in the army, an officer's uniform, now wore green overalls and a green shirt. And a hat. The hat was the worst. It looked like something you'd wear in the jungle. It had a long brim and a piece of material that flapped down from the back. "To prevent a sunburned neck," Sister Catherine told him.

The other day when Selina and I were outdoors with the kids, letting them run around, I saw my father in the distance, staring up at the sky. He did that a lot. One of the other counselors called him "the statue." "Wait till Sister Catherine catches him doing that," I overheard her say. "He'll be out on his ear."

I watched until he started to turn over the soil. With no gloves. He'd always worn them when he helped my mother in the garden, which wasn't often. My mother used to tell me his hands were set apart from the rest of his body. "Hallowed," she said. I watched him, dressed in those ugly overalls and hat, rubbing his sleeve over his forehead, and I wanted to cry.

Selina tells me it's the way things are for now. That I should be grateful he's working. That I should be patient. That even Sister Catherine is patient with him. Treena told me Sister Catherine said she is convinced God sent my father to the convent. "He's here not only to tend our garden but his—"

The morning flew by and, precisely at eleven-thirty, Selina and I were in Sister Catherine's office, waiting to be paid.

Sister Catherine was going through a pile of envelopes.

"If she doesn't hurry, we'll never make it," Selina said in a loud whisper.

"I heard that, Selina."

Selina got behind me.

"Aaah," Sister Catherine said, pulling two envelopes out of the pile, "here you are. You girls have earned this. Sister Pat tells me you're both doing fine work. However," she said, looking at Selina, then me, "no more of the ruckus that went on yesterday. No more Laurel and Hardy imitations. Is that clear?"

"Yes, Sister," Selina said.

Selina had done an imitation of Laurel that was so real, I'd almost forgotten it was Selina. She walked like him and twirled her hair and cried the way he does. "Sorry, Ollie," she'd kept saying. I'd played Ollie with a pillow under my shorts. The kids loved it.

As soon as we got outside, Selina opened her paycheck. "No wonder she said we earned this. Look at this puny amount. I'm fifteen years old and I'm paying Social Security. Do you believe that?"

"Come on," I said, "it's the law, and we're wasting time."

"We're lucky if we can afford a sandwich with this."

"So we'll split one," I said, taking her by the arm and dragging her along toward the road leading to town. "Stop complaining."

"Sure, Selina, stop complaining," she said, mimicking Sister Catherine's voice. "Work hard. Be grateful that I have seen fit to put a few bright copper pennies in your paycheck. A change of attitude is what's needed here. A sense of gratitude and thankfulness for the privilege of doing the Lord's work. Working with little ones is a gift—"

"One of these days she's going to hear you imitating her."

"Never. Haven't you noticed how deaf she is?"

"So how come she heard you this morning?"

"That's because she put a new battery in her hearing aid," Selina said, now running ahead of me. "Hurry up. I'm starving, and I heard that Caleb is there today."

I caught up with her. "Where did you hear that?"

"I have my sources," she said, running faster.

Bailey's was crowded, but there were two counter seats open. And there he was, wearing that stiff white uniform, making an ice-cream soda. He pumped syrup into a tall glass, poured in some cream, placed the glass under the seltzer spout, and stirred it all up. Then he put a scoop of chocolate ice cream on top. It was the most beautiful thing I'd ever seen.

Then, without looking in our direction, he said, "What'll you have?"

I could barely breathe.

Again without looking in our direction, he told us the two choices of the day were tuna on a roll or egg salad on whole wheat.

"Tuna on a roll," Selina said.

"Tuna on a roll coming up," he said.

Then he came and stood directly in front of me. "What about you? Tuna, too?"

"Hello, Caleb."

He kind of squinted, then said, "Tess?"

I nodded.

"Every time I see you, you look different."

"I do?"

"You do. Now, what'll you have?"

"Tuna."

"Tuna it is."

As he fixed the sandwiches, he asked us what we were doing with ourselves for the summer.

"Working at the convent as counselors," Selina said. And before I could stop her, "Tess's father took the groundskeeper's job."

"Full-time?"

I nodded. "But I think he's going to need a helper."

He spread mayonnaise on the rolls. "If he does, I'm available."

He put the sandwiches in front of us. "How come he decided to take the job? I thought you were on your way somewhere."

"We were." I told him how my father wasn't able to practice anymore.

"He's a surgeon?" He shook his head. "How about that?" He laughed. "Some pay cut."

"They're getting the apartment, too," Selina said.

"When are you moving in?"

"I'm not sure." My heart pounded in my ears.

"I know where I can hire out a truck if you need some help."

"Help?"

"Moving. Like Mayflower. Global."

"Mayflower? Global?" I asked, dumbfounded.

"Movers," Selina said. "He's teasing you."

"No, I'm not. I'm serious If you need help, I can get a truck."

He put the sandwiches before us and then went to the end of the counter to fix our vanilla Cokes.

"Boy," Selina said, "if my father owned all the businesses that his father does, I wouldn't be working the way he does. He must have five jobs. He probably could set his own hours working for his father."

"I think it's good to try to be independent."

She shrugged and took a bite of her sandwich. "To each his own, I guess. But I think it's a little crazy."

"Well, I think it's honorable."

Then I bit into the most wonderful tuna sandwich I had ever eaten, and the vanilla Coke slipped down my throat as smooth as satin.

That night, when my father and I took our walk, the full moon was so bright it was almost like daybreak.

My father told me he had called my mother. She was pleased he had taken the job. "I told your mother not to worry about us. To concentrate on what she has to do."

It was the first time my father had said anything like that. But I began to wonder if he was really thinking about her and Helen, or if he was thinking that he didn't need another person around to pressure him.

"What did she say?"

"We talked about my working at the convent." He shrugged. "I told her it seems I never catch up."

"You've only been there a few days."

He sighed. "That's true."

We walked to the lake without saying another word, and then I said, "Papa, what you need is a helper." I slipped my arm through his and began to walk toward home. "I happen to have a friend who needs a job. His name is Caleb and he would be perfect. Absolutely perfect."

Chapter Fourteen

The cashier at the hospital always says the same thing when anybody tells her good news. "It happened because you prayed," she'll say. "From your mouth to God's ear." Well, that happened to me. I prayed, and Caleb is going to be helping my father at the convent. He starts today. I still can't believe it. But all is not perfect. This afternoon Selina and I and the other counselors are taking the swimming test. Wearing the black, itchy bathing suits, with the white stitching on the back that says, PROPERTY OF COR MARIA CONVENT. *Selina said when wool bathing suits are wet, they will definitely stretch. "Stretch?" I said. And she said there was a distinct possibility they will shrink when they dry. Treena said we are young and beautiful and the suits won't be*

noticed, they will kind of disappear.
Wouldn't that be a hoot, as Clio always
says? The suits disappearing? Seven girls
standing there with a bunch of boys and
Sister Catherine and no bathing suits.
Cor Maria would never be the same.

"Oh, my God," Selina said as we headed toward the pool. "It's bad enough there are boys here. Does he have to be here, too?"

His back was to us, but it was Caleb. He was sweeping out the pool house. I wanted to run, to hide somewhere, but Sister Catherine ushered us down to the end of the pool where the swimming instructor waited. She introduced us to Mr. Conners, then told him to come back to her office when the testing was completed to give her the names of those who made lifeguard and those who would be pool helpers.

"Everybody into the pool," Mr. Conners said. "I want to see what you can do."

With my eyes on Caleb's back, I slipped out of my robe and into the water. Mr. Conners had us swim the length of the pool a few times and then told us all to get out, except Marie Doolcy. He told her to go to the shallow end and wait. Then he called Caleb over.

"What's he calling him for?" I said in a panic.

"I don't know," Selina said, clutching her cover-up.

Mr. Conners shook Caleb's hand. Then he said to us, "Sister Catherine arranged for Cal to help me out. Maybe some of you know him, but don't assume anything. For your purposes, he can't swim. He's drowning, he's scared, and it's your job to get him to safety."

He slapped Caleb on the back. "Go to it."

Caleb positioned himself at the deep end. He pointed his toes as though getting ready to dive, but hesitated. His skin shone in the sunlight like it had been oiled. His bathing suit was black and the way it fit I knew it wasn't the property of Cor Maria. He glanced around, then turned his back toward the pool and made the most beautiful backward dive I've ever seen.

Selina poked me. "Did you see that?"

"Show-off," one of the girls behind me said.

Once in the water, Caleb made it look as though he was in trouble. He sank down, then came up and yelled for help. Mr. Conners had instructed Marie she wasn't to make a move until he told her.

"Now, Marie. Get him out. Fast."

As soon as Marie hit the water, Mr. Conners called out Lee Ann Downes's name and told her to get ready, her target could be any one of us.

"Watch closely," Mr. Conners said, his eyes on Marie and Caleb. See if she gets him to safety. Watch what she does. Watch what he does."

Marie swam underwater and surfaced a few feet away from Caleb. She turned him around and put her right arm under his chin.

An uncomfortable feeling swept through me. Almost like jealousy. I'd never been jealous over a boy before. I watched as Marie, Caleb alongside her, paddled toward the shallow end with her other arm.

"Give her a hard time, Cal. She's getting off too easy."

Caleb slipped away from Marie, pretended to be going under, and pushed Marie away a few times. But she managed to get a grip on him and got him down to the shallow end.

Caleb lifted himself out of the pool with one beautiful motion, then turned and helped Marie.

"Showing off his muscles," Selina said.

I could feel my face redden.

Mr. Conners called Lee Ann and Carol Smythe. And me.

I stood up.

"Which one are you?"

"Tessa Ramsey."

"You start with a dive, and let me see how fast you can get to the shallow end. Lee Ann and Carol, you wait here."

No one else had started with a dive, except Caleb. I wanted to die.

I ran to the diving board and positioned my feet on the end of the board, glanced over to see if Caleb was watching—he wasn't—took a deep breath, and dove in. Surfacing, I heard the sound of bodies hitting the water, then Mr. Conners yelled, "Ramsey, your target is in trouble at the deep end, right side."

Swimming underwater I reached the deep end and my target. I grabbed his arm, then put my other arm around his neck, one part of me hoping it was Caleb, another part hoping it wasn't. It was.

I let go.

"Hold on to your target."

I put my arm back around Caleb's neck.

"You're drowning, Cal. You're scared."

Caleb pretended to fight me off. I could hear the rest of the counselors laughing.

"You'll lose him if you don't think fast."

I couldn't think. He flailed his arms and legs, and every time I tried to bring him in, he kicked harder.

"Please," I whispered. "Stop."

He did. For a minute. Then he started up again.

"I said get him in."

Grabbing him by the hair, I put my arm under his neck. I felt like my heart was coming out of my chest.

Caleb tucked his head into the curve of my shoulder and looked up at me. "You're beautiful," he whispered.

My legs felt as though they weren't part of my body.

"You are," he said. "You really are."

My arms went limp, and he slipped away from me.

"Get him in. Your target is going to go under."

I put my arm around Caleb's neck again and tried to bring him in, but I couldn't. I felt weak all over, thinking of what he'd said.

"Come on out, Cal," Mr. Conners yelled.

"Sorry," Caleb said, hoisting himself out of the pool.

"Why?"

"I think I made it too hard for you."

But I wasn't sorry. He'd said I was beautiful.

Mr. Conners asked me to do a few turns in the pool to see if I was a strong enough swimmer to be a pool attendant. Finishing at the deep end, I placed my hands on the pool's coping and took some deep breaths. I was about to swim over to the steps to get out of the pool when Caleb crouched before me. He put his hands under my arms and lifted me out of the water, holding me at arm's length as though I were a child.

"Don't let it get you down," he said. "You're almost as good a swimmer as I am. And almost as pretty."

He put me down. "Maybe I'll see you later."

I stood there immobile until Selina came over. "What happened? You're a better swimmer than I am. You could have taken him in."

I didn't answer. I slipped into my robe and sat down and let the heat of the sun warm me. I closed my eyes and imagined Caleb there with me, saw him lift me out of the pool, heard him say I was beautiful.

"You didn't make it, Tess."

"It doesn't matter."

"It doesn't matter?"

I shook my head. "He said—" I stopped, remembering that Selina seemed to like him, too.

"What did he say?"

"Tell me the truth, Sel. Do you like him? I mean *really* like him?"

She shrugged. "Like I like a lot of people. But definitely not the way you like him."

"Does it show?"

She rolled her eyes. "No, fair Juliet, not at all." She leaned toward me. "Now tell me what he said."

"That I was beautiful."

"He did?"

"He did. He said, 'You're beautiful. You are. You really are.'"

"And that made you cave in like that?"

I nodded.

"Well, Marie said it was unfair, and I agree."

"What's unfair?"

"That he gave you such a hard time," she said, taking some lotion out of her robe pocket. "I think he was showing off a little," she said, rubbing it on her arms and legs, then passing it to me. "At your expense."

"He was supposed to give me a hard time," I said defensively. "That happens. Somebody drowning would give you a hard time."

"Why didn't you sock him? That's what you're supposed to do if somebody is putting your life and theirs in jeopardy."

"Sock him? I couldn't do that."

"Well, I would have."

Mr. Conners called her name.

She gathered up her things. "And I'll tell you something. If he's my target, I'll do just that. Hard."

"Selina Maddox, into the pool. Now."

Selina put on her racing cap and headed toward the diving board. "Wish me luck."

I didn't see her make lifeguard. My mind left my body at the pool and went somewhere with Caleb. And he was telling me again how beautiful I was.

At home that night, Treena asked me if I felt all right. "You're so quiet," she said. "That's not like you."

"I'm fine," I said.

"How did you do today? Did you make lifeguard?"

"I'm a pool attendant."

"What about Selina?"

"Lifeguard. She and Marie Dooley are lifeguards."

And that night when my father and I walked, it didn't bother me one bit that he was so quiet. I was too busy thinking and imagining how wonderful the rest of the summer would be. Working with Selina. Swimming. Maybe some picnics. And, most definitely, Caleb.

Chapter Fifteen

❖

Mom called last night. She sounds lonely and sad, which is not like her at all. She asked about Papa and I told her he was doing okay, which isn't exactly the truth. Most days he seems distant. He can be standing alongside somebody and not be there. It's frustrating at times. Like the other day: He was weeding the flower bed under the window of Sister Catherine's office. I called out to him, not once, but five times. Finally Sister Catherine poked her head through the window and after she said something to him, he turned and waved. It hurts, too. Especially when some of the counselors make fun of him.

Mom told me Helen's baby was going to be delivered by cesarean section at the end of next week and that she had decided to take a quick trip down to see us. I may be wrong, but my father didn't seem really happy about that. He said he was, but he looked a little tense. I know he's having a hard time at the convent. Caleb must be working at Bailey's overtime because he hasn't been able to help too much at the convent.

We're to move into the apartment over the garages soon. I'm anxious to move in. As much as I love being with Treena, I want my own room. Treena has been great about sharing hers, but I think she'll be glad, too. Sister Catherine had three of the postulants paint the apartment. Selina and I are going over on Saturday to set things up, do some cleaning.

Selina's not herself. She seems preoccupied. Distant, almost. At first I thought it might be because of what happened at the pool the other day, that she really did like Caleb more than she was saying, but yesterday she told me it has nothing to do with that. It's her mother. She's getting restless, Selina says, which means she'll be wanting to move again. I would hate for Selina to move. I used to think I was close to Clio, but now I think it was just because we spent so much time

together. All we ever talked about were
things outside ourselves, like the movies,
or what other kids were doing, or school-
work. It's different with Selina, and I've
come to know it's not sharing time that
makes you close, it's sharing yourself.

"Tess," Treena called from the kitchen, "telephone."

"Hey Tess," a familiar voice said, "guess who?"

"Caleb?"

"The one and only."

My heart almost stopped. I hadn't seen nor heard from him since the day at the pool. It seemed he was always where I wasn't.

I took a deep breath.

"What are you doing tonight?"

"Working. Selina and I are working."

"Tonight?"

"No, today."

"I asked you what you were doing tonight."

"Oh, tonight."

"Are you okay?"

"Yes, I'm okay." I took another deep breath. "What about tonight?"

"I thought maybe you might want to go to the carnival."

"A carnival?"

"Yeah. There's one out by the lake. It opens tonight."

My heart sank. "I'd love to, but Selina is spending the night here."

"Oh," he said.

I said nothing, hoping he'd say something like "Bring Selina." He didn't.

"See you in church," he said.

"In church?"

"It's an old saying, like see you around, or see you later. You never heard that saying in Michigan?"

"Milwaukee. No, I never heard that in Milwaukee."

I didn't want him to hang up. But Selina told me I shouldn't try too hard, that I should relax and let him do the chasing. That that's what ladies are supposed to do.

I took another deep breath. "Maybe Selina and I can meet you at the carnival."

There was a long pause and then he said, "Sure. See you there."

Before I could ask him exactly where, he hung up.

When I told Selina that Caleb had called and wanted to meet us at the carnival, she said no. "I'll just be in the way."

"You won't. He asked especially for you to come," I lied. "Come on, Sel. You're the one who doesn't freeze up when he's around. I do. Please? I really want to go."

It took the better part of the day, me pleading with her, until she finally weakened and agreed to come.

We spent the afternoon at Treena's, planning what to wear, how we'd fix our hair. Even the toilet water we'd splash on became a problem.

"Jean Naté," Selina said. "It's subtle."

"Too lemony. What about White Shoulders? Treena's got some in the bathroom."

"White Shoulders? That's for old ladies."

After supper we finally agreed it would be Jean Naté or nothing. Taking one last look in the mirror, we said good night to my father and Treena and were on our way.

I was so excited, I didn't feel one pang of guilt for not being able to take a walk with my father.

The lights from the carnival lit up the lake. Yellows and reds. Oranges and blues. We looked for Caleb everywhere but couldn't find him. All we saw were people carrying huge stuffed animals, eating pizza and cotton candy.

Selina wanted to give up, but I convinced her to walk around one more time. "Maybe he's on one of the rides."

"I'll bet he's at one of the booths," she said. "Guys like to win things." She pointed to one of the stuffed animals. "Like that stuff. Maybe he's tossing some balls."

At the last booth, Selina said she was tired of looking for him and wanted to try her luck at winning. She lost. Then I decided to try and, to my amazement, I got three pins down.

The man behind the counter handed me a stuffed Winnie the Pooh about six inches high.

"Don't I win one of the big ones?"

"You got to play three games to win one of those. What do you think this is? I'd be out of business if I gave one of those for every one-shot deal."

"But it doesn't say that."

"Get lost, kid."

From behind me somebody said, "You cheated her.

She played fair, and you owe her one of the big ones."

It was Caleb.

The man told him to get lost, too.

But Caleb leaned over the counter and said, "She'll take one of the big ones or I'll report you. My father happens to be the mayor."

The man handed me a big one.

"Your father is the mayor?" Selina said. "I thought he owned Girard Electric and Girard Motors—"

"Shhhh. I just said that to scare him," Caleb said, guiding the two of us away from the stand. "Now what have you two been up to?"

I prayed Selina wouldn't tell him we'd done nothing but look for him.

"Have you been on the Zipper yet?"

"The Zipper?"

He pointed to a ride with lights that went up and down, making it look like a zipper being zipped. People sat in wire cages that rose high in the air and swung around and around at a dizzying speed.

"That?" Selina said. "You have to be crazy to get on that."

"How about you, Tess? You afraid?"

I was terrified. "No," I said. "It looks like fun."

Selina grabbed my arm. "Fun! Are you crazy? Do you know how they put those things together at these carnivals?"

I hesitated but before I could say anything, Caleb handed Selina the bear, took my arm and the next thing I knew, I was on the Zipper.

Once strapped into our two-person cage, I felt

"To the men's room. I'll probably never see him again."

"Would that be the end of the world?"

I nodded.

"You like him that much?"

"I do."

She put her hand on mine. "You'll hear from him. You will, I know it. Because if he likes you as much as you like him, do you think he's going to let something like this bother him—" She started to laugh again.

And even though I tried not to, I did, too.

Chapter Sixteen

Four days, four long days have passed since that awful night at the carnival, and I still haven't heard from Caleb. The day after it happened, he called Sister Catherine to tell my father he wouldn't be in. That he was sick. Imagine. I made him sick. He hasn't even called about the moving truck. Selina keeps telling me he will and if he doesn't, that it's his problem. That's easy to say, but I think I'll shrivel up and die if he doesn't call. Just the other day he told me I was beautiful. "You are. You really are," he said. And then I had to ruin it all. I called my mother and told her about it. She sympathized with me, but said not to let it undermine my confidence. That in ten years nobody will remember. Another easy thing to say. She told me that when she and my father were

dating, he took her to hear the Milwaukee Symphony Orchestra play at Lake Michigan. It was a warm summer night and she had bought a new dress for the occasion. They sat on the grass, and when intermission came, my father asked her if she wanted to walk down to the lake. She said she heard people laughing as they walked past, but she thought it was just from the sheer joy of being on Lake Michigan, the lake breeze cooling them off, a perfect evening. That is until my father got behind her. The back seam of her dress had opened. Because of the heat, she hadn't worn a slip and there she was, her dress blowing in the breeze, her panties in full view. "I thought it was the end of my life," my mother said. "But I'm still here."

Why do adults do that? Say dumb things like "Ten years from now, nobody will remember." Ten years is so far off, it doesn't matter if Caleb won't remember then. It matters that he remembers now. And he hasn't called. He never will. Who wants to be with somebody who did what I did? And to think the night it happened, I laughed about it. I don't think I'll ever laugh again. I'm ruined.

Selina and I are going over to the apartment this morning to start setting it *up. Just the small things, like dishes and stuff. Treena has been pulling things from the basement and the attic for us to use since we'll only be there temporarily—*

The kitchen phone rang, and I heard Treena say, "Fine. I'll tell her."

I leaped out of bed, grabbed my robe, and headed down to the kitchen. By the time I got there, she was outside in the garden.

"Who was that on the phone?" I called out to her, hoping, praying it was Caleb.

"Selina. I'm picking her up at eleven." She got down on her knees. "Come on out, it's glorious. And bring me some coffee, please."

That was the last thing I wanted to do, go out in the garden. I'd end up weeding alongside her.

But when I got to the garden, a mass of beautiful confusion, Treena's face was almost beautiful, too. At first I thought it was because the more I got to know her, to experience her goodness, the more I loved her. But no, it was more than that. She did look different. Her garden transformed her.

Without her asking, I got down beside her and pulled weeds along with her. Every once in a while, she'd brush her bare hands off on her overalls and take a sip of coffee. Her fingernails were black. As much as my mother loved to garden, she never dug in the soil with bare hands. She always wore huge white gloves that reminded me of a mime I once saw at the Milwaukee Children's Museum.

My father was sitting on the porch glider. Treena called to him several times to come out into the sun. "Give us a hand, Danny."

"Later, Treena, later."

"Always later," Treena muttered under her breath. She tossed the weeds she'd pulled into a basket set between us. "I'm giving him until the end of next week to see that psychiatrist."

"I thought you said it had to be in his time."

"Well, I'm changing my mind," she said, yanking out a deep-rooted weed. "And I've changed my mind about your moving into the apartment. I'm glad that you and Selina are getting it ready."

"You're tired of us, aren't you?"

"Good Lord, no. But I think the sooner your father is out from under my protection, the better things will be for him. I'm not helping him. In fact, I'm probably hindering him. That's not fair to your mother, or you. Maybe being on his own will nudge him into doing something. But if he doesn't—she sighed—"Who am I fooling? If he doesn't, there isn't a darn thing I can do about it."

She got up and picked up some tomato plants she had started from seed. "Help me stake these out, will you, Tess?"

It took a long time to stake the plants and put wire around them so the rabbits wouldn't get in. Every once in a while Treena or I would call out to my father, but he just sat there, staring.

"He should be helping you," I said.

Treena shrugged.

Standing there, hammering down one stake after another, I thought of what my father had said, about Treena being only eleven when he was born, how she had to take care of him and the house because his mother was always sick. Imagine being eleven years old taking care of a baby, doing housework. When he'd told me, I'd felt sorry for him because his mother hadn't been there for him. But he was like that, too. Even though he was here, he was never there for me, either. Now it was Treena I felt compassion for. I felt the anger in the pit of my stomach. I whacked the hammer hard, so hard some of the stakes split, and I drove one clear down to the ground.

Treena said nothing.

When the last bit of wire was in place, Treena and I went into the house to sort out the things for the apartment. "This way you'll have the kitchen set up before you move in. Then as soon as the plumber connects the water system, you'll be ready to go." She loaded dishes and silverware, towels, and pots and pans into cartons.

"Didn't you say that Caleb Girard was going to help?"

"I haven't heard from him."

"Why don't you call him?"

"I can't do that."

"Why not? Isn't he coming with a truck? We'll have to know the date. I've got a kitchen set and two beds down in the basement. Plus a sofa. Chairs. If he's not able to do it, we've got to get somebody else. Call him."

"I don't know his number."

Treena took the telephone book from the rack.

"Girard, 742 Garfield Street . . . 555–7803." She handed me the phone. "I'm going to make some lunch. I'll pack some for you and Selina."

"Hello," I said to the lady who answered. "May I speak to Caleb?"

"Sorry, m'dear, but he's not here. He's been away for a few days. Who's calling, please? May I take a message?"

"This is Tessa Ramsey, Mrs. Cooper's niece. Could you have him call me? The number is 555–1777. And if I'm not here, I'll be at the convent. In the apartment. Would you tell him that?"

"I surely will. Bye-bye."

"Thank you. Good-bye."

"What did he say?" Treena asked. "Is he coming?"

"He's not home. He'll call when he gets home."

"We'll give him until Tuesday," Treena said. "If we don't hear from him by then, we'll get somebody else."

Opening the refrigerator, she took out a plate of ham, then turned to me. "Wait a minute. I seem to remember your father telling me Caleb had called in sick."

I was hoping she wouldn't remember.

"That's odd," she said. "But predictable."

"Why do you say that?"

"Oh, nothing. It's just that as bright as Caleb Girard is, he tends to be a little irresponsible." She bumped the refrigerator door with her hip to close it. "But then again, he was only a sophomore when he was in my English class, and I'm such a perfectionist when it comes to my discipline, it's probably an unfair judgment." "Ham and cheese or cold chicken? Or both?"

"Both." She handed me two slices of bread. "Why don't you fix yourself some toast and peanut butter? I'll bet you haven't had anything to eat."

I slipped the bread into the toaster and looked at my reflection in its shiny surface. "My hair is terrible since I came here. It's so flat."

"It's the hard water. Why don't you use some of my rollers? They'll give it some bounce."

I showered and set my hair, picked out a clean pair of shorts and top, then combed out my hair. I looked like Harpo Marx. I tried brushing it until my scalp was sore, tried to get it into a ponytail, but it just popped out. I gave up.

As soon as Selina got in the car, she said, "Well, that does it."

"Does what?"

"With that hair, you'll never be able to play Ollie to my Stan. The kids will never believe it."

Treena laughed out loud. "It's not that bad. It looks like it's going to rain one of those hard Taloosa rains, and that should take care of it."

After helping us carry the dishes and things up to the apartment, Treena said she'd be back to pick us up about five or so. "I'll be tutoring all afternoon."

"This is nice," Selina said, walking from one room to the other.

And it was. My father had told me he'd already picked out his room, the one next to the kitchen. It was small and not particularly bright, but the other bedroom, the one that was to be mine, was perfect. It faced southeast and was sunny, and the south window looked out on the tower. I loved it. The living room was pleasant, too, even though four of them would have fit in our living room at home. There were bookcases, and it even had a small fireplace.

I could hardly wait to move in. I was tired of writing in my journal when what I wanted to do was talk. I wanted to stretch out on my bed, Selina beside me, and talk about everything and everyone. Especially boys. One boy.

Selina found a step stool and started in the kitchen. She put pots and pans away and found room for the dishes in a corner cabinet. She washed everything before she put it away, even the already clean silverware.

I did the bathroom. Put fresh towels in the cabinet and hung a curtain Treena had given me. The window was high and shaped like a half-moon. I imagined what it would look like when the moon shone through. A moon within a moon.

We washed the insides of the windows and swept out the fireplace, and after we piled my father's books in his room, we decided to eat.

Selina wanted to go to the tower. "It's cool up there."

We climbed the hill, Selina shouting all the way that Rapunzel still lived and that her prince would come anytime now to rescue her.

By the time we reached the tower, it began to rain a soft rain.

"God answered your prayer," Selina said, trying the tower door. "He sent rain." She tried the door again, but it was locked. "Wait here," she said. "I know a way in."

It had to be twenty degrees cooler inside. The stone

walls were thick, with high, narrow windows. The floor was brick, and a narrow, winding staircase circled up to another level, and another, ending at a platform so high, my neck hurt from looking up.

"Look at that," Selina said, pointing to a carefully folded blanket and a picnic basket exactly like Treena's.

"Treena must have bought hers in the same place."

"I don't mean the basket. I meant I was right about somebody being in here. Lovers. And one of these days I'm going to find out who they are." She laughed. "Maybe it's Mr. Conners and Miss Sydell."

"That's a terrible thing to say. He's married."

"I'm only kidding. It's probably some kids. Walter Desmond or somebody."

"Who's Walter Desmond?"

"That jerk in Bailey's. The one who dripped Coke down my back that day."

Thinking about that day make me think of Caleb and it made me sad. "I still haven't heard from him," I said.

"Who? Oh, *him*," Selina said, spreading out the blanket Treena had tucked inside the basket. "Marie Dooley told me the senior girls say he thinks he's God's gift to women."

"I agree."

"She also said that his father was the one who got him appointed to West Point."

"So what does that mean? And why is Marie so interested in him?"

She shrugged. "I don't know."

"She probably has a huge crush on him, and he

doesn't know she exists."

"Forget it. Let's eat. I'm starved."

We ate all the sandwiches and part of the chicken, then leaned back on the cool stone walls, sipping sweet tea.

Selina closed her eyes.

"You tired?"

"Mmn-mmn. I'm imagining the lovers who meet here."

"You're nuts."

"He's tall, but not too tall, with wild curly hair, great muscles, and smooth olive skin." She looked at me and laughed. "Who does that sound like?"

I gave her a gentle shove.

"And the girl. She has long straight hair—"

"Like Rapunzel?"

"No. Shorter. With bangs. When they dance . . . they dance a lot . . . she stands on his feet—"

"Barefoot, or does he wear shoes?"

"Don't get technical." She poured herself more tea. "Did you ever kiss a boy?"

"Not really."

"What do you mean not really?"

"Well, there's this boy, Francis. Francis DeVine—"

"Is he?"

"Is he what?"

"Divine."

I laughed. "Well, he thinks he is. In one afternoon at the movies, he kissed every one of the girls."

"How did it feel?"

"Like nothing, except maybe disgusting."

"Sloppy, I'll bet. Wet and sloppy."

I nodded. "My friend Clio told me she kissed Henry Silvers once. She said it was wonderful. His lips were just moist enough. And his breath was okay."

"That must be the worst. Bad breath. Yuk."

"Clio told me she read that Clark Gable had the worst breath in Hollywood. That his leading ladies hated to kiss him."

"How does she know that?"

"Her father owns three movie theaters and he gets all the movie magazines for nothing. She knows everything about everybody in Hollywood."

"Like what?"

"Like anything you want to know about your favorite movie stars."

"For instance."

"For instance, she told me that Gregory Peck was an only child and that his parents were divorced when he was ten and that he lived with his grandmother. That he liked the beach—"

"And his breath was awful and he had false teeth. Teeth." She looked at her watch. "I almost forgot. It's after three, and I've got a dentist appointment in ten minutes. I've got to go."

"I'll call Treena. She'll drive you."

"No. It's not that far. It'll take me less time to run than to wait for her to come." She handed me the rest of the chicken. "I'll call you tonight, okay?"

Back at the apartment I was just about to call Treena when somebody knocked on the door. I thought it was Sel. "Did you miss the appointment?" I called out.

"I didn't know I had one. It's me, Cal."

As always, my heart pounded, skipped, almost stopped. "Hi," I said, opening the door.

"Hey, every time I see you, you look different."

I smoothed my hair down. "It's my hair."

He laughed. "You look like you stuck your finger in an electrical socket."

"What?"

"Like you were electrocuted." He smiled that wonderful smile that made my knees weak. "I know, you never heard that in Minnesota."

"Milwaukee."

"Sorry, Milwaukee."

"How are you feeling? I heard you were sick."

"Oh, yeah. I was, but I'm fine now." He came into the kitchen. "My mother told me you called."

I wanted to ask him where he'd been, but I didn't dare. Instead, I asked about the truck. "Treena wants to know. She has some heavy pieces for us to move."

"The truck? Oh, yeah, the truck. I'll try to get it for Saturday. Is that okay?"

"I don't know. I think we were going to do it before then."

"Let me work on it." He glanced over at Treena's picnic basket. "Where did that come from?"

"It's Treena's. Selina and I had a picnic."

"Oh."

"We went up to the tower. In fact, we ate right in the tower."

"How did you get in?"

I shrugged. "Selina got us in."

"Oh," he said again.

"Would you like some cold chicken?"

"Sure, but I don't like it cold. Could we heat it?"

"I'm not sure how to work the stove."

"I'll show you," he said, pressing a button and turning a knob. *"Voilà."*

"Do you like your chicken hot or very hot?"

"Medium hot."

I felt foolish babbling on the way I was. Hot or very hot. It was what happened when I was with him. My heart pounded. My legs abandoned me. I said stupid things. And then there was the Zipper.

"I'm sorry about the other night," I said.

He shrugged. "Things happen, but you should have told me you don't like rides. It would have been okay. In fact, it would have been more than okay. That whole thing freaked out a lot of people."

I could feel my face redden. "It's just that I didn't know how much I didn't like rides. My aunt said some people can't take motion or the bouncing."

He picked up a chicken leg and in two or three bites, it was gone. He reached for another. "I had your aunt when I was a sophomore. She was tough." Another chicken leg disappeared. "But she was good. In fact, my father wants her to tutor me in Latin."

"Really?"

"I'm going to West Point, and he, my father that is, thinks I should brush up."

"Do you want me to tell my aunt?"

He shook his head. "My father thinks I should brush up, not me."

After all the chicken was gone and everything was cleared away, he asked if he could walk me home.

Forgetting about Treena, I said yes.

Taking my arm, he guided me through the orchard, across a field, and then to a road I'd never been on.

"This is the long way to your aunt's, but the best way," he said. "So, tell me, how do you like it here?"

"I like it a lot. Especially knowing Selina." And then, in the tiniest voice, "And you."

He didn't hear me.

"So when did you meet her?"

"The first day I came. I was walking by the tower, and there she was. She told me there are lovers that go there. Like Rapunzel and her prince."

"She's got a wild imagination," he said.

Then he asked me about my father. He couldn't understand how a surgeon could take the job as groundskeeper.

I found myself telling him about my father and Vietnam.

"Anybody who served there has got to be crazy."

"My father is not crazy."

"I didn't mean that. What I meant to say was it was a crazy war. I mean, it wasn't even a war war."

I wanted to ask him what it was if it wasn't a war, but I didn't want to start anything I'd be sorry for, so I changed the subject. I asked him about West Point.

He told me how hard it was to get an appointment, and all about what plebes have to go through. That he was sure he'd measure up, but he hated the fact that he'd have to be in the service for so long after graduation. "Maybe I'll go into medicine. Like your father." A strange feeling came over me when he said that, as though somewhere deep inside of me I knew he was going to say it before he said it.

He took my hand. My heart skipped.

The road was dusty, the sun high in the sky. We walked side by side next to a field of tall yellow-green grass that swayed with the breeze; tiny birds flew over and under. Caleb talked all the while.

I began to think how strange it had been since leaving Milwaukee. It was such a short time ago, and yet in many ways I felt at home here in this funny little town. I thought how strange it was to be here with Caleb. He was eighteen years old, almost a man. I'd just turned fifteen.

"Tess," Caleb said, waving his hand in front of my face, "you're spacing out. Am I talking too much?"

"No," I said, "you're not talking too much."

He grinned. "Hey, that's almost too good to be true. Some people think I do. Talk too much, that is."

Maybe it's all too good to be true, I thought. Too good to last. Coming to Treena's. Meeting Selina. Then Caleb. Being able to stay—

"Hey," Caleb said as the sound of thunder rolled across the field and a streak of lightning quickly followed, "let's move."

He took my hand again and we ran down the road until we came to a hill that Caleb said led to Treena's. The sky opened and the rain came down in torrents, soaking our clothes; gusts of wind whipped across my face. We climbed the now slippery trail, sliding back in the mud so many times, it felt as though the hill had become a mountain. When we finally reached the top, I could see Treena's house below.

Caleb stopped by a tree, lifted his hand, and cupped my chin. "You're beautiful," he said, as though he hadn't said it before. Had forgotten.

"No, I'm not," I said. "My mother is much prettier."

"She must be a real Miss America, then." He moved his hand to my cheek and rubbed my lips with his thumb.

My chest felt as though it would explode. I didn't know I could feel like this, a feeling so strong it frightened me, a feeling that maybe I couldn't control.

"I feel happy with you, Tess," Caleb said. "Sometimes I think I'm basically an unhappy person, somebody who expects too much. But with you it's different."

"But you hardly know me."

He shook his head. "I know you." His eyes were steady on mine. "I think we were in another life together."

I felt limp all over. As though I were in a dream and everything was speeded up. My body, too. "We'd better go," I said, stumbling over the words. "I just remembered I was supposed to call Treena."

My back was against a tree, his arms circling me. He pressed my hand to his face and kissed my palm. Then my cheek. My nose. I couldn't get my breath.

"We had to be in another life together," he said. "Yeah. We probably lived high up in the Sierras—"

"I should go."

"Or down by the sea. I like that better. Maybe you

were a mermaid and I was Moby Dick and I swallowed you whole. . . ."

"I've got to go." I slid under his arm and stepped away from him. "I really have to."

"Okay," he said, smiling broadly, taking my hand in his. "I like that. A mermaid and Moby Dick." He kissed each of my fingers and then we started down the hill, tripping over roots, slipping on pebbles. He squeezed my hand gently as the rain beat down on us, and suddenly I wanted the hill magically to turn into a mountain, one so tall we'd never reach the bottom, so we could just keep running like this, Caleb's hand clutching mine, forever.

Chapter Seventeen

Sometimes I feel like I'm living in a soap opera, like "The Guiding Light," or "As The World Turns," where everybody has huge problems. Where lives are schizophrenic. One day the characters are on top of the world. The next day they've plummeted to the depths. The only difference between their lives and ours is that they have wise, live-in grandfathers who always know the answers and make things come out okay. We're not that lucky, Selina and I. Just the other day I was feeling so good about everything. Caleb had walked me home, told me I was beautiful again, told me so many things, and then he disappeared for days, coming and going to the convent like a phantom. Then my father started acting strange about my mother coming down to visit. "Don't feel that you have to," I heard him say the other night. "I'm doing fine." Well, he's not. He hasn't been sleeping, and his smoking is getting worse. Even though most of the time he smokes outside, the smell from his clothes permeates the inside air.

And then there was yesterday with Selina. Yesterday was awful.

The temperature was about 110, and we wanted to go into the pool but didn't have our bathing suits. Treena was at a meeting and the walk back to her house was too long. Selina said she'd check with her mother and maybe we could go to her house. "I've got two decent suits," she said. "No Cor Maria stitched on them." Selina called her mother, supposedly to see if she could pick us up. She let the phone ring for a long time, but there wasn't any answer. Selina said she had the key, so we could go there. It was the first time Selina had ever asked me to go home with her.

We cut up some construction paper to make visors to shield our eyes against the sun and started out.

We took our time, stopping at every public drinking fountain to cool off. We passed the Thomas Alva Edison High School. Selina told me the boys there had pierced ears, wore kerchiefs around their heads, and went to school on motorcycles. Her mother had refused to let her go there, even though getting the money for Cor Maria's tuition was hard for her. Her mother wanted her to be a lady. Passing the Homestead Bar and Grill, Selina told me her mother worked there as a cook four nights a week.

At a dusty road with a sign reading FARLEY'S BUNGA-LOW COLONY, Selina announced that we had arrived. "We're the last one in the court." Once at the door, she knocked, then waited a while before putting her key in the lock.

She poked her head in and called out to her mother. No answer. She called out again, waited, and then motioned for me to follow.

We made our way through a narrow hallway, the floor painted red. Dark green carpeting covered the narrow stairs leading to the second floor. The kitchen was dismal, except for the refrigerator that was painted bright yellow. Inside there was nothing except half a bottle of ginger ale, two shrunken apples, and a cracked cup with a dried-out tea bag in it.

"My mother can make a thousand cups of tea with one tea bag," Selina said. She laughed. "She's a cook, a good one, too, but she never has time to do it at home."

"Who's that?" a voice called.

Selina froze.

"We'd better go," she said, slamming the refrigerator door. A woman appeared in the doorway, her starched red hair matted, her thin legs bare, her arms clutching a frayed cotton robe around her. "What are you doing home?" she said. "Why didn't you call?"

"I did."

"Belle," a man's voice called, "where the hell are you?"

Selina looked over at me. "Let's go."

"Wait, Sel," her mother said. "It's not what you think—"

"What is it, then?"

"George was just helping me paint the place. Honest." She smiled over at me. "You want some iced tea, hon?"

I shook my head. "No, thank you."

"It's good for you on a day like this." She looked at

Selina. "Make some iced tea for your friend, Sel." Then, turning to me, she said, "She makes it good."

Selina headed toward the back door. I followed. Her mother ran ahead and stood in front of the door, her arms stretched out. "Wait. Where you going? I'll get George to drive you. He was just leaving."

"Belle," the man's voice called again, "you coming back, or are we through?"

Selina's face reddened. "Come on, Tess." She turned and ran across the painted red floor and out the front door. I followed.

"I'm telling you, hon," her mother cried out, "he was just helping me paint. I swear to God."

Selina kept running.

We ran, the sun at its hottest, and when we couldn't run anymore, we took shelter underneath the portico of the Thomas Alva Edison High School.

Selina stood with her back to me. I thought she was crying and didn't want me to see her. But she wasn't.

I wanted to reach out to her, to say something to comfort her, but words wouldn't come. I thought about her mother. How sad she looked when she saw Selina and me in the kitchen. How thin her legs were. How she wanted Selina to go to Cor Maria and not to this place. To make a lady out of her. I felt like crying.

Selina started to shiver, even though it was so hot out, the heat from the cement burned through the soles of my shoes.

"Come on, Sel, let's go. You're going to get heat-stroke if we stay here."

"I hope I do. I hope I die of it."

"Don't say that. Don't you ever say that again."

Selina's shoulders sagged, as though they were weighted down. "It's strange what they teach you, isn't it?"

"What is?"

"That God gives you free will, but He knows ahead of time how you're going to use it. It doesn't seem right, does it?"

"What do you mean?"

"Well, if He knows what you're going to do, and it's going to mess up your life, why wouldn't He change things? Give the person a break?"

"I don't know why it's like that," I said, surprised I'd never thought about it before. "When you think about it, how can somebody be born and already their whole life is there? No matter what happens, it's . . . it's—"

"Preordained."

"That's it. Preordained."

"I think it's dumb," she said. "People can change. They don't have to mess up their lives. If God is what I think He is, I think maybe He gives people a push in the right direction."

"Maybe. Or maybe the person was going to go that way anyway."

"My mother's not a bad person. She's messed her life up a lot, but she's not bad."

"I know that."

Selina's voice was caustic. "You just met her. How could you know that?"

"Because you're her daughter. And anybody who has a daughter like you isn't bad. It just doesn't happen like that."

She turned to me. Her eyes glistened, but no tears came. "Thanks," she said.

I slipped my arm through hers. "I've got a dollar. Come on, we'll get a drink to cool us off. Okay?"

We haven't spoken about what happened, but I keep thinking about it, about her mother, about how much Selina has come to mean to me. How awful that day must have been for both of them. It made me think of something I thought about my own mother when I was about five. I thought she was in love with the mailman, so I told the people my mother worked with that she had a boyfriend. I still remember the look on my mother's face when I said that. "What are you talking about?" she said. "What boyfriend?"

"The mailman," I answered.

My mother tried to explain that she knew the mailman from school days. That she gave him cool drinks, and on the hottest of days, she invited him into our kitchen.

My mother told my father, and they laughed about it. "They probably believed her," my father had said. "Kids tell it the way it is."

I wish I could do that now. Tell it the way it is. Tell my father to stop moping around, stop feeling sorry for himself, stop ignoring me and my mother. Treena, too.

I wish I could tell Caleb how I feel. How confused I am about him. One day he tells me I'm beautiful. And then he disappears. But I know I won't. I guess I'm a little too old a kid to do that.

Chapter Eighteen

My mother is coming this week-
end. I can hardly wait. I've told her all
about Selina and I'm anxious for them
to meet.

When I told her what happened
at Selina's the other day, all she said was
that it's hard bringing up a child alone.
That it was lonely and sometimes overwhelming. And then she said, "Seems to
me you've made a good friend. Maybe
even your best friend, like Helen is mine."

I just know she's going to like
Selina. My mother liked Clio a lot, but I
know she didn't care too much for her
mother. She never said so, but from the
time Mrs. Howland told me her ancestors
came over on the Mayflower and asked
me how mine came over, I kind of knew.
I remember Papa telling me I should tell

Mrs. Howland that his ancestors came over on the May Flower. His grandfather was in love with a Miss May Flower, who owned a boat named after herself, and the two of them took off one day and landed at Plymouth Rock.

I'd forgotten about that, forgotten that Papa ever said anything funny.

What I'd really like to forget are some of the things Selina has been telling me about Caleb. Marie Dooley is the official keeper of Caleb's comings and goings. From Marie to Selina to me. Marie thinks she knows everything about everybody, including Caleb, and Selina thinks it's her duty to tell me. First she told me Marie said most of the girls think he has an ego as big as the state of Texas. And then Selina added something of her own. Something about his not recognizing me, always telling me I look different.

Then, as much as I know it's all heresay, it got me to wondering about the day he said I was beautiful. Not the day at the pool, but the day he said it again, as though it was the first time he'd said it. And then when he said I made him happy, that was strange, but then I got to thinking that someone with a big ego wouldn't say that. It's something somebody who isn't sure of himself might say.

And as far as him not recognizing
me . . . well, hair does do certain things
to people . . . makes them look different .
. . and I do tend to fix my hair lots of
ways . . . especially the other day when I
curled it . . . I kind of did look like Harpo
Marx . . .

Putting my journal under my pillow, I headed out to the porch and joined my father. Our walking had become a ritual. No matter what I was doing, except for the night I went to the carnival and I'll never do that again, I knew when it was time for our walk. We started exactly at seven and came back exactly at eight. We talked a little. About nothing most times. I asked if he likes his job as groundskeeper, or if he'd had enough exercise, or did he want to stop for an ice cream, and if he did, what kind did he think he'd have. The ice-cream parlor we'd discovered was not far from Treena's. We talked about the tables and how small they were. How cold the marble tops felt when we rested our arms on them. How the scrolled metal chairs were good looking but not very comfortable. How the lady behind the counter was so thin. And how did she do it with all the temptations?

Tonight would be the same.

My father was on the porch, just sitting.

"Are you ready?"

He nodded.

After a few minutes I asked him how he was feeling.

"A little better," he said. "And you?"

"I'm doing fine," I said.

"Good."

"I like it here, Papa."

He smiled a very small smile. "Papa," he said. "That name always made me feel so old."

"Is it because that's what Mom calls her father?"

"I suppose. But I've grown into it."

"You're not old."

"Old enough."

"Too old to walk all the way down to the lake?"

"No."

"No, you're too old? Or no, you're not too old."

"Not too old."

"Good."

We walked silently, the trees murmuring in the small breeze that blew up from the lake. The lake is the lake again. No carnival rides. No noise. It's as though I am walking homeward toward Lake Michigan.

"I can't wait to see Mom," I said. "I miss her."

An odd expression came over my father's face.

"She's not coming," he said.

"Not coming? But last night she told me she was."

"I spoke to her just before we left."

"What did she say? Helen can't do without her for two days? I'm calling her. She's coming."

He stopped walking. "I asked her not to."

"Why would you do that?"

He sighed. "Helen needs her. She may deliver—"

A sudden, overwhelming anger came over me. I thought about Selina and her mother. How whatever her mother does affects Selina's life, whether she wants it to or not. How my father has affected our lives. My life. And he's doing it again.

"That's not why," I said. "You're afraid. Afraid she'll be another one to tell you what you have to do. How much you need help."

"I told you I'd get help."

"But you haven't, have you? You just say you will. You don't do it."

"I will. Didn't I ask Treena to find somebody?"

"She did, but you didn't go."

"Tess, let's go back. I'm tired . . ."

"So am I. I'm tired of worrying about you. Tired of you being tired. Tired of lying awake waiting for you to have another nightmare. Tired of hearing about that boy—"

An expression washed across my father's face that frightened me. He held his hand to his chest as if in pain.

"Are you all right?"

He didn't answer.

"I'm sorry," I said, putting my hand on his arm. "Let's go back."

He didn't move. He stood as though his feet had taken root. He took a long, shaky breath and said in a voice just above a whisper, "He was just a kid." He sighed a long, wavering sigh.

Suddenly I didn't want to hear anymore. "Stop," I said. "This is upsetting you."

But he didn't. He told me how every night, as soon as he puts his head on the pillow, this boy calls to him. As soon as sleep comes, he feels the heat of the jungle, sees the boy walk to him through the mist. My father's eyes met mine, but they stared right through me, as though I was invisible. Tears fell down his cheeks, across his lips. He spoke slowly, almost whispering. "He's not moving, just standing in a pool of water, that damn mist rising up, surrounding him, but no matter how heavy the mist gets, I see him. . . ."

"Papa, stop."

He looked around as though he heard something, then began again. "I tried. I tried hard." A sob took hold of Papa's whole body. "I'm sorry. So sorry . . .'"

"Please, Papa, no more. You're upset—"

But he didn't stop. His whole body shook, but somehow his voice got louder. Clearer. "He keeps coming toward me, relentless, just like them. 'It was too late,' I tell him. 'Don't you hear what I'm saying? You had no pulse. Your stomach was blown apart. Goddamnit, boy, you were dead when they brought you in.'" He stopped and wiped his forehead with his sleeve. "I prayed to God you'd breathe. I bargained . . . if only you'd breathe. I did that. Bargained . . . but when they cut away your pants . . ." He stopped, his body rigid. "Oh, God," he said, panting, looking toward the lake. "Dear God, help me. Get me home."

Chapter Nineteen

"He's going to be fine," Treena said as we walked down the hospital corridor. "Stop blaming yourself."

"I shouldn't have said what I did."

"Stop that. You did something he couldn't do for himself. Now he'll get help, so don't punish yourself."

"He looked so awful."

"He looks worse than he is."

"Tell me again what the doctor said."

"He's going to see your father every day."

"For how long?"

"I have no idea."

"I've got to call my mother."

"I already have. She's on her way."

"When will she be here?"

"Probably by morning. I assured her your father is going to be all right. He'll be in the hospital for a day or two at most—"

"A day or two? But what about his heart?"

"There is nothing wrong with his heart."

"But I was there. He couldn't get his breath. He just kept holding his chest. He was choking."

"His heart is fine. He hyperventilated. It sometimes happens when someone is under stress."

"Then it was my fault. I shouldn't—"

Treena stopped walking and took my hand. "Last night was a gift, Tess. You did exactly the right thing for your father. You forced him to open up. Now it's time you do something for yourself.

"You two will move into the apartment just as planned. The doctor feels it's the best thing for him. He wants him to keep working at the convent. He wants me to stop coddling him."

"Does this doctor know what he's doing?"

"Oh, my God," she said. "You sound like an old woman. Yes, he knows exactly what he's doing."

"I don't know about that—"

"Well, I do. And I know this . . . you've got to let go. I've got to let go and let somebody less emotionally involved take over." She gave me a quick hug. "Come on, Tess, your father is going to get better, and so are we. For starters, we're going home and sleeping until noon."

"Tess? Is that you?"

My eyes barely open, I mumbled, "Yes. Who is this?"

"It's me, Selina. You were supposed to call, remember?"

"What time is it?"

"Eleven. We were supposed to finish up the apartment."

"My father is in the hospital."

"Hospital? Why? What happened?"

I started to tell her, and then from out of nowhere, I began to cry.

"Oh, Tess," Selina said, "I'm sorry."

Treena threw the covers off. "If that's Selina, tell her to come on over. The day is going as planned."

"I heard her. I'll come right now if you want me."

I nodded, as though she could see me.

"Tess? Do you want me there?"

"Yes."

"Your father will be okay. I know it. Do you hear me?"

"I hear you," I said, half believing her. "I hear you."

As soon as Treena left the bedroom, I dialed the hospital.

I waited and waited and when I was finally put through to my father's nurse, I asked to speak to him.

"Sorry," she said, "Dr. Nolan is in with Dr. and Mrs. Ramsey. Why don't you try a bit later."

"Was that the hospital?" Treena stood in the doorway, sipping her coffee, wearing the same overalls and boots as the day we came.

"My mother is there."

"Come on, then. Get dressed and come out and have some breakfast. I've got the best store-bought biscuits and raspberry jam in the county."

And then, as though she read my thoughts, she said, "Tess, things will get better. Your father is going to make it. He will."

I heard the screen door bang and Selina's voice float down the hall. I dressed quickly and within minutes I was sitting at the kitchen table, Selina beside me, Treena at the stove making more coffee. I wished time would stop for a while and when it started up again, everything and everyone would be in place, and things would be just fine again.

Sitting with my mother in the cafeteria, waiting for Treena to pick us up, I told my mother I wasn't going back to Milwaukee with her. "I'm staying here, and so should you."

My mother shook her head. "You didn't hear one word I said, so I'll repeat it. Dr. Nolan said it would be best for your father to work this out with him, somebody familiar with postwar trauma." She leaned back and rubbed her temples. "Without ever having met me, he knew me. Knew I'd try to be your father's therapist. Knew I'd try to make everything better. Knew I'd slow up his recovery."

"That's a terrible thing for him to say."

"It's true, Tess. I know that. So don't give me a hard time about leaving. It's been as hard on me as it's been on anybody."

I leaned over and put my hand on hers. "I know that and I'm sorry. But I need to stay. I'll do as the doctor says. I won't interfere. I promise I won't do anything that's not good for Papa."

"Easy to say, hard to do. Have you any idea how difficult living with somebody going through intense therapy can be?"

I shook my head. "Easier than what it's been. At least he'll have somebody to talk to."

"But what about you? Who do you talk to?"

"There's Treena. And Selina." And Caleb, I thought.

"It scares me to think of what might have happened if you hadn't had the good sense to come to Treena's." She sighed, leaned back, and rubbed the back of her neck. "Your friend Selina is a lot like her."

"So am I. Let me stay."

"It's not fair to burden you with all this. I never should have agreed to let you go in the first place."

"He needs me. He'll be lonely."

My mother flew back to Milwaukee the day my father was released from the hospital, but not before the three of us had a conference with Dr. Nolan. We were to move into the apartment, my father would see the doctor every other day and would be responsible for taking his medication. My job was simply to take care of myself. "Nothing more," the doctor said. "Leave him to me."

Chapter Twenty

We're finally moving into the apartment today. We were supposed to move in last Saturday, but the bathroom sink backed up and flooded the bathroom. Sister Catherine called the plumber, but he told her the sink was beyond repair. He said he had a slightly used one in his garage that wouldn't cost her much more than if he'd been able to repair the old one. Sister Catherine asked Papa if he could pick it up, and so he and Treena are on their way to Scokee in the convent truck and as soon as they get back, we're moving. Flood or not. Sink or not.

It's rather amazing to me that Papa agreed to drive to Scokee. In a truck. That he's up to all that. But these last couple of weeks, he's been conscientious about seeing the doctor and he seems a *little better. Maybe it's talking about it or maybe it's the medication. Whatever it is, I'm grateful. He's still withdrawn and quiet at times, but the quiet part seems different. More introspective, rather than simply not there.*

He talks to my mother, and once in a while I can feel his tension. I think he feels guilty that he's relieved about her decision to stay in Milwaukee even though Helen had the baby—a beautiful girl, my mother says—Nola Esmond Traynor. My mother says she'll visit, but she is determined to give Papa the space he needs to work his way through things. Treena says once we move into the apartment, maybe she'll change her mind. I doubt it. It's funny, I thought I'd be furious with her for not coming as soon as Helen had the baby, but I'm not. Maybe it's because I think she's right. Or because I'm happy here with Selina. And Caleb . . . he's going to help us move. He can't get the truck, but he said he'd be here to help this afternoon. When I told Selina, she asked me how much he was going to charge. I told her she should stop listening to Marie Dooley's gossip about him. "Think for yourself," I said. She told me she always thinks for herself. She can be a pain at times.

❖   ❖   ❖

"We can't wait all day," Treena said, loading another box onto the pickup truck. "It's after four and if we don't get started, it will be dark before we're half done."

Selina had one of those I-told-you-so looks spread all over her as she carried carton after carton out of Treena's.

"I didn't say a word," she said as we crossed paths on the porch. "Did I?"

"You don't have to. I know exactly what you're thinking."

"Just what you're thinking. Where is he?"

"He'll be here."

"So will Christmas."

Caleb didn't arrive at the apartment until we were unpacking the last of our things and were about to sit down to Treena's picnic supper. He apologized for being late. He said the other counterman hadn't shown up for work and Mr. Bailey asked him to fill in. He tried to call but got no answer. I believed him, but Selina rolled her eyes and gave me a "tell-me-another-one" look.

Treena asked him if he wanted to stay for supper. He did. I tried to hold a conversation, tried to include everybody, but I finally gave up. My father looked as though he was falling asleep and hardly said a word. Treena and Selina were quiet, too. Caleb just ate. Every once in a while he'd look up and wink at me. I lost my appetite. Why is that? Why, when my stomach was calling out in hunger, one look, a wink, and I couldn't eat a thing?

Right after supper my father excused himself. Treena did, too, but not before asking Caleb to help her home with some things we decided we didn't need.

Selina said he looked relieved to be getting out of it so easily. That he could have come back and helped set up the living room. She makes me so mad sometimes and then she does something that makes me feel bad about being mad. Like giving me a present for my room. A beautiful scented candle in a crystal container. It's not real crystal but it shines as though it is.

After she left I took a bath. I put the bathroom light out, lit the candle, and put it in front of the moon-shaped window. I saw a crescent moon outside. So strange—two moons, one real, one not. I wondered about the person who made the window. A romantic, probably. Maybe the same romantic who built the tower. I stayed in the tub a long time. I always showered at Treena's and it felt so good to be in a tub, letting the water run until it covered my whole body. My body— sometimes it frightens me. These feelings I have when I'm with Caleb. Even when I think about him. I remember what the health teacher back in Milwaukee said... "These feelings are natural, normal. But remember, there are consequences when young people give in to them. . . ." I stayed in the tub until the water ran cold, then I dried myself carefully and put on the dusting powder Treena had given me, blew out the candle, and got into bed.

Chapter Twenty-one

❖

I can't believe we've been in the apartment almost a week. I love it here. Especially this room. In the morning the sun streams from the east window and across my bed. And from the south window I see the tower. It was so funny. Papa has been working at the convent for weeks now and had never noticed the tower. "What's that?" he asked me the other day when he was adjusting the window. When I told him, he just shook his head and said something about his head being in the clouds at times.

As much as I love it here, I miss Treena. At times it's awfully quiet with just the two of us. We talk, but there are times when I know he wants to be alone with his Camels. Last night was different. He knocked on my door and asked if he could come into my room. He sat in the rocking chair and rocked for a while. He told me he felt comfortable with Dr. Nolan, and he appreciated my staying. Then he asked how things were with me. That really surprised me. I told him I was fine. I thought he was going to ask me about Caleb, too. He hasn't said anything, but I don't think he likes Caleb. He answered the phone the other night when Caleb called to tell me he had to work at Bailey's and we wouldn't be able to go to the movies. I heard Papa say something to Caleb about being more responsible about coming to work at the convent. Papa never could understand why people didn't live up to their commitments.

But last night he didn't ask about Caleb. He just sat there rocking, his head back, his eyes closed. After a while, he said good night and told me he was going outside to smoke.

I'm confused about how I'm feeling about Papa. I always wished he was more like Clio's father, like Atticus, and now it seems I don't think about it so much anymore. Is that part of growing up? I don't know. I hope so. I think it started the day Caleb told me he wanted to be a doctor . . . but why? Am I afraid he'll be like my father, or afraid he won't be? I *really don't know what I'm thinking. . . .*

Anyway, tomorrow is the day the campers are having a picnic. Caleb will be there, too. Sister Catherine asked him to do the cooking. Selina said how wonderful it was that Caleb would do anything for Sister Catherine. And then added, "for money, of course." She still doesn't understand why he works at all. She keeps telling me his father has a ton of money, and I keep telling her I think it's admirable of him to be working when he doesn't have to. . . .

"Who here knows how to light charcoal?" Sister Catherine asked when it became obvious Caleb wasn't coming.

Selina volunteered herself and me.

"The least he could have done was call her," Selina said, crushing newspaper and stuffing it under the coals.

"Since when are you so concerned about Sister Catherine?"

Bending over to light the newspapers, she shrugged and said, "The kids are hungry. And I can use the money."

"What money?"

"The money she was going to pay Caleb."

"She's not going to pay us," I said. "We'd have to be here anyway."

"Oh, well," she said, fanning the flame, *"c'est la vie."*

We cooked thirty-two hot dogs and twenty-five

hamburgers and when we were finished, we drank a gallon of lemonade, stuffed our pockets with giant chocolate-chip cookies, and headed for the pool.

Marie Dooley was there with Lee Ann, waiting for the campers to come down for their swim. The air was still, the pool's surface like glass, the only movement a trail of ripples made by a family of ducks skimming along its surface.

"Aren't you the lucky one, Sel," Marie called out. "You get out of baby-sitting the kids. I should have done the cooking."

Selina waved. "I hate when she calls me Sel."

"Why? I call you that once in a while."

"You're different," she said, holding on to me while she wriggled out of her shorts.

"I should hope so. She's such a gossip."

Throwing her shorts off to the side, Selina turned her back to me and stretched out her arms. "Ta-da. The property of Cor Maria is taking a long swim."

"What about the ducks?"

"They won't mind," she said and jumped in.

The ducks kept swimming.

"Come on in," she called. "There's room."

We swam for a while and when we were tired of trying to swim around the ducks, we laid on the warm cement. A light, warm breeze drifted across my face and, ignoring the shouts and splashes, I dozed off.

Selina's voice woke me, but I pretended I was still asleep.

"Isobel? Isn't she the one who was two classes ahead of us?"

And then Marie's voice. "That's the one. Blond curly hair, at least it was blond and curly before she went into the convent." She sighed a deep sigh. "I feel so bad for her."

And then Lee Ann. "But it's true. Why do you think you haven't seen her in a while?"

"Sister Catherine, or somebody, said she was on retreat."

"You are so gullible, Sel," Marie said, her tone haughty. "I saw her in town yesterday. With him."

"Who is him?" Selina asked.

Still pretending I was asleep, I opened my eyes just a slit. Marie looked all around before she answered in a loud whisper, "Caleb. Caleb Girard. That's probably why he's not here today."

I sat up and turned to Selina. "What is she talking about?"

"One of the postulants is in trouble," Selina said.

"So what does that have to do with Caleb?"

Selina shrugged and looked away.

"Who do you think you are?" Marie said. "Too special to talk directly to me? Well, I can do that too. Sel, tell her that Caleb was seen with her and—"

"I'm not a puppet," Selina said. "Talk to her yourself."

"Exactly what do you think that means, Marie?" I said. "That he was seen with her?"

"That he probably was the one."

"The one?"

"The one who got her pregnant," Marie said.

I felt as though she had slapped me. "What a horrible thing to say."

"I'm just telling you what everybody is saying—"

"And who is everybody?"

"Everybody is everybody."

"You're nothing but a gossip. A filthy gossip."

"I'm sorry if I offended you, Miss Proper Tessa Ramsey. Sorry if I offended your delicate ears. Sorry that I offended your beloved . . . or the one you think is your beloved."

"You're a liar, as well," I said.

I grabbed my towel and started toward the pool gate.

"Wait," Selina called, running after me.

"How could you sit there and listen to them? How could you?" I pushed the gate open.

"Did I say I believed it?" Selina said, taking my arm.

I pulled away.

"Take it easy. You know how Marie is."

"The eyes and ears of the world is what she thinks she is. Only she doesn't realize she's blind and deaf to what's really going on."

In the distance I heard somebody call my name. I turned and saw Caleb running toward us, waving his towel over his head like a flag of surrender.

I waved back.

"Be careful, Tess," Selina said.

"You *do* believe Marie, don't you?"

But before she could answer, Caleb was beside me, asking me to go down to the lake with him, the lake where we'd first met.

Without saying good-bye to Selina, I slipped my arm in his and started down the tar path.

Chapter Twenty-two

It was so hot, the tar stuck to the bottom of my sandals and threw me off balance. I tried to stop myself from falling, only to have my knees and palms hit the ground hard.

"Are you okay?" Caleb asked, helping me over to the grass, sitting me down.

My knees and palms were scratched and raw, my sandals caked with tar. I was so embarrassed, I felt my face color.

Caleb knelt beside me and, with the end of his shirt, tried to wipe the tar from my knees. Then he took my hands and held my palms to his cheeks. "You scared me," he said.

My knees hurt but my palms, resting on Caleb's cheeks, felt cool.

"I'm sorry," I said.

"For what?" he said, kissing each palm, his eyes fixed on mine.

My mother always said there is always one part of

every person's face that seems to reveal them exactly. With my father it was his eyes. And now, looking at Caleb's, I realized how much he reminded me of the picture Treena had showed me of my father when he was fifteen. Except for the eyes—

"Hey," Caleb said, "I asked you what you're sorry about."

"For being so clumsy." Then looking at my knees, "I really should wash this stuff off."

"Hey," he said, jumping up, "how about if I get the mower and drive us down to the lake? You can wash off there."

He was halfway up the hill before I could answer. Even though my knees were killing me, I felt happy. Light. I lay back, closed my eyes, and pushed away all that I'd heard down at the pool. "Gossip," I said aloud. "Nothing but gossip."

When Caleb got back, he helped me climb into the seat beside him. Sitting there made me think of the first day I'd met him. How he almost ran me down with the mower. How scared I'd been. How I'd left my shoes. . . .

"Hey," Caleb said, heading toward the road leading to the lake. "Let's get into the lake fast. That okay with you?"

He didn't wait for an answer but put his foot on the gas. Hard.

I gripped the side of the mower with one hand, my other hand on the back of the seat, thinking about how he had had trouble stopping the mower that day. He left the road and roared across the grass. "Want to go right into the lake in this?"

"No!" I screamed.

"Just kidding," he said.

"Slow down."

But he didn't. We bounced over tree stumps and went around boulders and shrubs. When we got to the top of the hill leading to the lake, I remembered how he had told me the lake was very deep in certain parts.

"Stop it!" I screamed. "Slow down!"

"I'll bet I can stop this tank two inches from the lake," he yelled over the sound of the motor.

The mower coasted down the hill, me screaming, terrified, him laughing, shouting, "Two inches. This baby can stop on a dime."

And then he braked.

"Hey, how about that? Two inches. Didn't I tell you she could do it?"

I was so angry, I didn't answer. The first time with the mower and the night on the Zipper, I'd told myself that he was fearless and I was filled with fear. But this time was different.

"You weren't scared, were you?"

My heart was racing. "Yes, I was scared. And I think it was a stupid thing to do."

"Hey," he said, "all I wanted to do was get you down here fast so you could clean yourself up."

He jumped out of the mower and came around to my side. "I'm sorry," he said, holding his hand out to me. "Come on, let me help you."

He looked so remorseful, my anger melted. I reached out and took his hand. He circled my waist with his other arm and lifted me from the mower. I felt the beginning of something happening deep in my chest. Almost like something had opened, let go.

"I'd better get this stuff cleaned off before it gets infected," I said, wiggling out of his embrace.

I walked over to the edge of the lake and put my hands into the cool water. Caleb came up behind me. "I've got a better idea. Why don't we go for a swim? That way you'll soak off all that tar. If you rub it, it's going to get into those cuts.

"Come on," he said, stripping down to his bathing suit. "The water's great."

Without thinking of the Cor Maria bathing suit I was wearing underneath, I slipped out of my shorts and top. Caleb took a running dive. I followed. "Where's the deep part?" I called out to him.

"Don't worry, I'll watch for it."

He swam over to me. "Nice, isn't it?"

"It feels so different than a pool. It smells more like the water at home."

"Minnesota has lakes?"

"Milwaukee. Milwaukee has Lake Michigan."

"Oh," he said, slipping his arm around me. "I'm not much for geography."

"I like it. I like knowing about where people live."

"What's it like in Milwaukee?"

"Cold. Some winter days it can be minus thirty-eight."

He turned my back toward him and drew me close. My head rested on his shoulder. "I don't think I could survive minus thirty-eight," he said. His breath was warm on my shoulder.

"You'd get used to it."

"I could get used to this," he said.

"What?"

"This," he said, kissing the crook of my neck, whispering how good it was to have me with him.

I knew if I had been standing I would have fallen, that's how weak my legs felt. A pulsing started deep inside me, moved down, scared me. I pulled away and swam toward shore.

"Tess, don't go that way. That's the deep end."

I panicked. I tried to stand but couldn't. I went under, came up, went under again. I pushed my shoulders up for air. I couldn't get my breath. I tried to swim, but my legs wouldn't move.

"You're okay," Caleb said, coming up beside me. "Relax. Hold on to me and we'll go back in. You'll be all right."

Once onshore, I calmed down, took deep breaths, thanked him for bringing me in.

"Hey, don't try that again. You were lucky you didn't get into the weeds. That's a tough place to get out of."

He put his shirt around my shoulders and stretched out beside me. "Look at the sky," he said. "It's cloudless. We usually have foul weather when we're together."

He reached over and brushed the hair away from my face. "What did you pull away for?"

I shrugged, ashamed to tell him.

"I wouldn't take advantage of you, Tess. You know that."

I nodded. "I know."

We lay there for a long while, holding hands, looking up at the sky.

I felt so happy being with him. Marie was a terrible gossip, and Selina had no business repeating what she'd said—

"Hey," Caleb said, "I'm getting hungry. How about you?"

"No. I ate so much at the picnic, I don't think I'll ever be hungry again."

"What picnic?"

I sat up, confused. "The campers' picnic. It was today."

He whacked his forehead. "I forgot. I did. My mother is giving this huge party, and the lady who was taking over samples of tablecloths never showed. I had to drive her to the showroom. She even ordered a tent. Ever seen one of those tents?"

"Only in the movies."

"Well, you're going to see one for real. You're coming to the party."

"A party? For what?"

"For me."

"Why?"

"I told you—West Point. Remember?"

"When is it?"

"A week from Sunday."

"Oh, I don't know."

"What do you mean, you don't know? I'm inviting you."

"I don't have any of my clothes here."

He turned my face toward him. "Don't worry about it. Come in that bathing suit if you want to."

"Be serious. Is it formal?"

He shrugged. "Everything my mother does is formal.

Breakfast is formal, lunch. You name it, it's formal."

"I have a long skirt."

"Perfect."

"Maybe I can buy a dressy blouse."

"Anything you wear will be perfect. You'd look good in rags."

He lay back down again. "So, was Sister Catherine angry?"

I shrugged. "Selina and I took over the cooking."

"How'd it go?"

"Okay. At least we didn't have to baby-sit the kids at the pool. Marie and Lee Ann got stuck with that."

"The yentas?"

"The what?"

"Yentas." He smiled. "They don't say that in Michigan—"

"Milwaukee."

"They're gossipmongers, those two. I heard they were passing around some stuff about me. Stuff that isn't true."

"That's what I told Selina."

"Selina was there?"

"Yes."

"So what did you tell her?"

"That what Marie said wasn't true."

He sat up. "What did she say?"

"Selina didn't believe—"

"Not Selina, Marie. What did she say?"

"Just some stupid stuff."

"It was more than stupid stuff, I know that. But it's not true."

"I know that. And that's exactly what I told them."

I reached out and put my hand on his arm, but he pulled away, then quickly said he was sorry, told me he wanted to tell me everything. The truth. That he trusted me.

"I never touched that girl. I'd never do that." His voice softened. "It's important that you believe me.

"It's like this. My buddy, the one I took over for at the convent, he got her that way. Then he took off, left her. What was I supposed to do? Turn my back when she asked for help? She couldn't go to the nuns, couldn't go to her parents. Neither could I. I couldn't go up to my father and say, 'Hey, Dad, my buddy got Isobel pregnant and then took off for parts unknown. How about giving me a few hundred dollars so she can get an abortion—"

"An abortion?"

"What else?"

"She could have the baby. Give it up for adoption."

He shook his head. "You don't understand."

"I do. My mother arranges that all the time. She could go up to my mother's clinic . . ."

He shook his head again.

"She could," I said.

His eyes narrowed. "How could she?"

"My mother can find her a place to stay until she has her baby."

"What kind of place?"

"There are homes, private homes that take girls in. And there are people who could adopt the baby."

"You mean your mother would do that for somebody she doesn't even know?"

"Yes."

"And nobody would report it?"

"No."

"I don't know. Isobel is afraid that people will find out."

I shook my head. "The clinic maintains a strict code of privacy. Nobody would find out from them."

"Really?"

"Really."

He put his arms around me. "You're special," he said. "So special."

He drew me close and just as his lips touched mine, a line of lightning cracked the sky.

The sky opened up and by the time we gathered our things and got the mower back to where Caleb had taken it, we were soaked.

Caleb wanted to wait it out, but I wanted to get back to the apartment. Wanted to call my mother so she could start working on everything. We ran through the field and across the road and when we got to the path leading to the apartment, Caleb cupped my chin in his hand and told me again how special I was. Told me he would tell Isobel. How she'd be fine because of me. Then he kissed me.

My whole body pulsed.

"You are something," he said and kissed me again.

I knew if I stayed my feelings would take over, so I turned and ran down the path, pretending he was beside me, just the way I had that first time.

My father was standing at the foot of the stairs to the apartment and when he saw me, he called out, "What kind of fool is that young man to take you down to the lake in weather like this?"

"How did you know where I was?"

"Selina called. And what's got into you that you'd go along with him?"

Again that feeling about my father came over me. Guilt, I guess. Because all I could think of was Caleb.

Chapter Twenty-three

❖

Before I could get in touch with my mother, Caleb called to tell me Isobel wanted time to think it over. That he can't push her into anything, that he has to wait until she makes the decision herself. How could she just go off like that? What would she tell her parents? That was days ago and I haven't seen him since. He's busy all the time. At Bailey's, getting ready for the party his mother is giving, sometimes at the convent. I don't understand it. I don't understand a lot of things.

Like last night. My father was up most of the night, smoking. Pacing around the apartment. I tried talking to him, but after a while I gave up. He was totally into himself. It's so funny, the other day he wanted to know where I'd been and why I'd gone to the lake with Caleb, but since *then it's as though I've disappeared.*

My mother said more than likely he is working his way through some painful things. Reliving Vietnam and the feelings that are surfacing are probably unbearable, more so than when he dreamed about it. "You keep on doing what you've been doing, Tess," she said. "Let your father work things out with Dr. Nolan."

I used to struggle with feeling guilty if I didn't walk with my father every night. Or if I thought he was sad. And now I feel guilty because I don't feel guilty about those things any more. It's crazy. . . .

I called Selina to tell her about Caleb's party. She started up with me again. "You're going to be hurt," she said. "Marie is a gossip, but maybe—"

"She's more than a gossip. She's a slanderer."

She tried to say something, but I didn't give her a chance. "You see him differently because of Marie. He's not like that. He told me everything—"

"Like what?"

"I can't tell you."

"He made you promise?"

"It was my idea, not his. And I don't want to talk about it anymore."

"Okay," she said, "I'll stay out of it. I've got enough of my own problems to worry about. See you tomorrow."

When I got to work, Selina was in the arts and crafts room, filling plastic cups with paint, clipping paper to easels. She hardly said good morning. She reminded me of my father. There in body only.

After we settled the children at the easels, telling them they had to take turns, she said she had something she wanted to tell me.

"If you're going to tell me again not to go to the party, don't. And if it's anything else about Caleb—"

"Why do you think everything has got to be about him? Sometimes I think you believe there's no one else in the world."

"And sometimes I think you're not really telling me the truth."

"About what?"

"Sometimes I think you more than like him."

She rolled her eyes. "Trust me, it's not like that at all." She turned and told one of the boys to stop pushing the girls, and then without turning back, she said, "It's about me. And let me finish before you start interrupting. Promise?"

"Promise."

"I've been thinking about joining the convent."

"You in the convent?"

"You said you'd listen until I finished."

"But, Sel—"

She held up her hand. "I've been thinking about it for a while. Remember I told you I feel more at home here than I've ever felt anywhere?"

"Yes, but . . . sorry, I won't interrupt again."

"Well, that's about to change. My mother wants to

move on. I'm tired of it. I'm not going to go from place to place, school to school, friend to friend. I don't want my life to be just one more life. I want it to be mine. To do what I want—"

"But you're only fifteen. How can you know this is what you want?"

"I know what I don't want."

"That's no reason."

"That's not the only reason."

"You mean God has called you?"

She shook her head. "Not exactly."

"Well, I think that's what's supposed to happen," I said. "My friend Clio's cousin joined a very strict order in Minnesota, and when her family asked her why she chose it, she told them that God not only called her, He told her where to go."

"Maybe that's not the only way He does it."

"What do you mean by that?"

"Maybe He speaks to different people in different ways. Maybe He sent me here, knowing what I'd want to do. That it was His way of calling me. His way of telling me where to go."

"That's ridiculous. You can't stand Sister Catherine, and you'd hate not being free to do what you want to do."

"Sister Catherine's okay, and maybe being free isn't all that great."

"Do you know what you're saying? I remember seeing a picture with Audrey Hepburn. She joined the convent, and what she went through was awful. They cut her hair off—"

"That's not the worst thing that can happen to you."

"It wasn't the worst thing. It was the loneliness. She was made to feel everything she did was a sin—wanting to see her family, talking to her friend—"

"I need to belong someplace."

"It's not the place that's important, it's people." I reached out, wanting to touch her. "Look at us. We don't agree on everything—"

"Here you go again with Caleb—"

"That's not what I was going to say. What I was going to say was even though we don't agree on everything, we're friends. We belong, don't we? I want to be able to see you, to be able to talk to you—"

"So do I. But you'll go on to Savannah as soon as your father is better. Or you'll go back to Milwaukee—"

"Or maybe I'll stay here."

She shook her head. "That won't happen. He's just not right for you, Tess."

"There you go—"

"But it's true. You're going to get hurt."

"You're wrong about him."

"I don't know about that."

"That's your opinion. I told you that when you called last night."

"It's not only my opinion—"

"There you go again. You accept everything Marie tells you, as though she's the only person who never tells a lie. Can't you think for yourself?"

She looked at me for a long, long minute. "Forget it," she said. "Forget I tried to tell you anything. About him. About me. Because all it ever comes down to is him. Him. Him. Him." She turned and with her back to me said, "I won't ever mention him again. I promise you that."

Then she went over to one of the easels and put her arm around one of the boys. "Hey," she said, "you are one terrific artist. You'll probably grow up to be another Leonardo DaVinci."

I tried calling Selina tonight, but got no answer. I feel sad about what happened this morning. And I feel sad about her wanting to go into the convent. And then I feel angry because of the way she acts sometimes. Like she's my mother instead of my friend. She's wrong about Caleb . . . I know she is . . . he called tonight. I asked him about Isobel, but he said she was still thinking things over. . . . I hope she decides to trust my mother. . . . The party is tomorrow. I'm a little nervous about meeting his parents and his other friends. I want to look sophisticated, so when Treena took me shopping, I picked out a white satin blouse. She's letting me wear her pearls. She didn't say too much, but I got the impression she wasn't too happy about my going. . . . I kind of think she and Selina have talked about it. . . .

My father forced himself to talk at supper. I can tell when he does that. . . .

The moon is almost full. I can almost picture Caleb standing below my window, calling to me. I remember Miss Ayer, my sixth-grade math teacher, telling us that daydreaming would get you nowhere. I disagree. It takes you everywhere. Everywhere you want to be. Because now, I am out in the moonlight with Caleb. He takes me into his strong arms and speaks my name. "Tessa. Tessa," he says, his lashes sweeping across my cheek. His lips part a tiny bit, and then he kisses me. I hear music and feel as though I can fly above the trees through the clouds, past the stars and into forever. . . .

Chapter Twenty-four

✦

Selina called this morning. I thought she was going to start up again about the party, tell me not to go. She surprised me. She didn't say a word about the party or Caleb. She's keeping her promise, and it makes me feel terrible. Some of what she said, especially my believing that Caleb is the only person that exists, got me thinking. Is that why I don't feel guilty about not walking with Papa anymore? Why I don't feel so lost when Papa's not there for me?

Last night my father asked if he could come into my room again. He talked a little bit about how Dr. Nolan told him it takes time to put something like a war into perspective and get on with your life. "I hope he's right," he said. And *then, just before he left my room he turned and said, "Tess, whether it shows or not, I'm trying." That made me sad. Am I so wrapped up in my own things that my father thinks I don't know that he's trying? But that's what Dr. Nolan said I should do, let my father work out his own stuff. Shoulds. There are so many shoulds. It made me think of what my mother used to say. Should and ought are synonymous with guilt. "You should be more thoughtful." "You ought to write that letter." What am I doing here? Who do I think I am? Sigmund Freud? . . . I've got to get ready . . . Caleb is coming at five-thirty and it's a quarter to five now . . . I'm glad I spent the morning in the tub . . . did my nails and toenails. Even rinsed my hair with vinegar. I borrowed Treena's rollers, but didn't do what I did last time. Just rolled up the ends. . . . Hope it comes out the way I want it and I hope I'm not the youngest one at the party. . . .*

"Tess," my father called, "telephone."

I threw the journal down and ran down the hall.

It was Caleb. I could hardly hear him.

I took the phone into the bathroom and closed the door.

"The party's off," he said.

"What?"

"I said there's no party."

"No party? But you said everything was set up. Ready."

"It is. But I'm not going."

"But isn't the party for you?"

"It is. But I'm not going to be there."

"Why?"

"I don't want to talk about it."

"Why not?"

"It's too complicated. Believe me, it's better we don't go."

"I don't understand."

"I'll explain when I see you."

"Then I'm still seeing you?"

"Sure. But don't say anything to anybody about this."

"I won't."

"You get dressed just as if you were going to the biggest party you've ever been to, okay?"

"Okay."

"I'll be there at five-thirty, just like we planned. Be ready."

"I'm almost ready now."

"Great. I've got my sister's car."

"Oh."

"What do you mean, oh?"

"I thought you and your father were going to pick me up. Didn't you say that?"

"That was before."

"But what will I tell my father?"

"What do you mean?"

"My father is still planning to pick me up after the party. That was the plan."

"So he'll still pick you up."

"But if we're not going—"

"Either we'll be back at my house before eleven or you'll be home before your father leaves to pick you up. Quit worrying, will you?"

"It's just that my mother really likes to know—"

"Your mother isn't here," he said, his voice on edge. "Hey, do you want to go out or not?" He paused. "Are you there?"

"I'm here. It's just that back in Milwaukee—"

"Forget Milwaukee. This is Taloosa. See you in half an hour."

Back in the kitchen my father was sitting at the table writing. When he saw me, he stopped.

"I was writing you a note to tell you I was going to see Sister Catherine."

"It's Sunday. You don't work on Sunday."

"She called me this morning and asked me to go down after vespers." He looked at his watch. "They're over at five, aren't they?"

"I think so. What does she want to see you about?"

He shrugged. "I just hope it's not about my job. I don't need another change right now."

He got up and headed toward the door, then turned. "Don't leave for that party until I get back. I'd like to see you off."

Getting dressed, I thought about the party. What could have happened? It was on, but we weren't going? Maybe it was because of me. His mother hadn't invited me. He had, and maybe she didn't like that.

I decided to push everything out of my mind and

concentrate on getting dressed. I slipped on the blouse, the satin cool and smooth against my skin. Putting the skirt over my head, I thought of my mother the day my father came home, how she wanted to look perfect for him. I glanced in the mirror and ran my fingers across Treena's pearls, surprised at how pleased I was with what I saw. My hair looked fine, just enough curl. Just enough makeup, too.

I couldn't make up my mind what shoes to wear. Flats or little heels? I chose little heels, even though they weren't the most comfortable shoes I'd ever had. Checking myself in the mirror again, I turned around and around, wondering what Caleb had planned now that we weren't going to the party.

Then I sat in the living room and waited for him. Looking around I realized my father had cleaned the apartment. The floors were shiny, and there was a Mickey Mouse glass filled with daisies on the fireplace. My mother would have loved that. He'd even pinned the lace curtains back, letting more light in. I wasn't aware he had done this.

Hearing footsteps coming up the stairs and thinking it was my father, I opened the door. It was Caleb. He was breathing hard.

"What's the matter?"

Between breaths he told me the car had been stalling. "I don't want to turn it off. I've got to take it to a gas station. I think my sister put some cheap gas in it." He reached out and took my hand. "Come on, Tess."

"But my father wanted me to wait—"

"He'll understand. Honest, Tess, if I shut the motor,

that's it." He smiled that wonderful smile, the one I wanted to believe he smiled only for me.

I'd never lied to my father or mother, and now, as much as I tried to convince myself that it was just the circumstances, I felt awful.

But even feeling that way, I picked up the pencil and as though somebody guided my hand to the paper, I wrote:

> *Papa, I'm sorry we couldn't wait, but there was a problem with Caleb's sister's car. I'll see you at eleven . . . remember the directions to Caleb's are on the counter. . . .*
>
> *Love, Tess*

And then, remembering the daisies on the fireplace,

> *Mom would love Mickey Mouse holding the daisies. . . .*
>
> *— T.*

Chapter Twenty-five

The truck swerved around the curve so fast, I didn't realize what happened until we were at the bottom of a hill.

"Caleb? Are you all right?"

"That damn idiot. He was so close he ran me off the road." He got out of the car and walked around to the front. "My sister is going to love this."

"Is it okay?"

"It seems okay. All except the front tires. They're wedged in tight. I'll never be able to drive it out of here without tearing them up."

"What will you do?"

"Send a tow truck in the morning," he said, getting back into the car. He sighed. "And I wanted tonight to be perfect."

"It was," I said, thinking of the dinner we'd just had. "Just perfect."

"Was it?"

I nodded and leaned my head back. "All of it. The

food and the candlelight and the music. . . ."

"Music? You call that music?"

"Yes. I happen to love Big Band music."

"But the jukebox kept skipping."

"It didn't matter."

And it didn't. It was like being in a movie, the light from the candle flickering between us, Caleb telling me how special I was, even listening to the stale joke the waiter told us.

"You hear the one about the kleptomaniac?"

Before we could answer he told us. "This lady kleptomaniac is seeing a big-shot doctor who tells her any time she feels like she's going to swipe something, she's got to call him. So one night she goes to this big fancy party—"

Caleb winked at me. It was the first time I'd thought of the party.

"You know this story?" the waiter asked.

Caleb shook his head.

"—anyway, the lady feels like she's going to steal big time, so she calls the doctor." He looked over at me.

"You know what he tells her?"

"No."

"Take two ashtrays and call me in the morning." He walked away, laughing at his own joke.

Caleb put his elbows on the table and leaned over to me. "Is that what your father tells his patients?"

"He would never say that," I said. It was the first time I thought about my lying to my father. But the thought left quickly when Caleb reached out and put his hand on mine and told me how good it was to be with me—alone . . . better than any party.

A sizzle swept through the air, and the sky got very bright, the kind of brightness that sometimes comes before a storm.

"Hey, what is it with us?" Caleb said, putting his hand out the window, checking for rain.

None came, but I could hear the sound of far-off thunder.

"Well, we can't just sit here," he said, taking a flashlight out of the glove compartment, checking his watch. "It's only a little after eight, and I don't want your father to know that we didn't go to the party."

"I know."

"Come on," he said, tucking the flashlight in his pocket, "it'll be okay." He put his arm around me. "You know what we can do?"

"What?"

He turned and pointed out the rear window. "We can go on up there, to the tower. That way, it'll only be a short walk to the apartment, and you'll be sure to get there before your father leaves to pick you up." His voice was gentle, reassuring.

Getting out of the car, he took my hand and we walked up the hill and across the field leading to the tower. Once there, Caleb told me to wait, that he would go in the back way, then open the door for me. It didn't occur to me then to wonder how he knew his way into the tower.

When he finally opened the door, he had the flashlight under his chin. Its light distorted his eyebrows and made his nose and mouth look ominous. "Enter," he said.

"Put that away," I said. "You look terrible."

He closed the door behind me, shutting out the light.

"Come on," he said, shining the flashlight up the stairs. "There's more light up there."

He took my hand and led me up the winding stairs to the second level. The light was dim, the windows high and small. He laid out a blanket he had taken from the car. "There," he said, sitting down, guiding me next to him. The beam from the flashlight made a circle like a full moon above us.

Caleb moved closer and put his arm around me. "Relax," he said, nestling his chin on my shoulder.

I felt his breath on my cheek. The whole of me quivered.

His lips touched my neck, my cheek. He buried his face in my hair. "Your hair smells like the sea," he whispered. He took my face in his hands. "My little mermaid." His lips were inches away from mine.

Afraid my whole body would let go, I said the first thing that came to me. I asked him if he knew the story of Rapunzel.

"Who?" The expression on Caleb's face changed quickly.

"Rapunzel, the girl who was locked in the tower."

"What are you talking about?"

"Didn't you ever read fairy tales?"

"No."

"What did you read?"

From the way he shifted around I could tell he

was irritated. "Comic books. Things like that."

"I loved fairy tales."

"Girl stuff."

"No, it's not. My father told me he loved them when he was a boy."

"My father would have keeled over if he saw me reading them."

"Well, then, I'm going to tell you one." He started to say he really wasn't into all this, but I went on. "Once upon a time a husband and wife in a little town in Germany wanted a baby. When their wish was finally granted, the wife spent days looking into her neighbor's garden that was filled with rapunzel—"

"I thought you said Rapunzel was a girl—" He moved closer, put his hand on my knee.

"It's a plant, too. Anyway, when she saw the rapunzel she wanted some, but the neighbor was Mother Gothel, a bad fairy. Everybody was afraid of her. So in the dark of night the husband went into the garden and tore out some rapunzel and brought it to his wife. She was so happy, she ate every last bit of it—"

"I'd like to eat you," Caleb whispered. His lips were close to my ear, his breath blowing bits of my hair onto my face. I kept talking.

"The next night the husband went into the fairy's garden again because the wife said she would die if she didn't have more rapunzel. But Mother Gothel was waiting for him. 'Before you can have more,' she said, 'you must promise to give me the child your wife will soon bear.' Afraid his wife would die, the husband agreed. In time, the wife gave birth to Rapunzel, who grew to be a beautiful girl, with golden hair that grew to her feet—"

"You've got a way to go," Caleb said, ruffling my hair.

I moved my head to the side and shook my hair free. "Don't you want to hear what happened?"

"Not particularly."

As though I hadn't heard him, I told him how Mother Gothel put Rapunzel in the tower and when she visited her, Mother Gothel would stand below the window and say, "'Rapunzel, Rapunzel, let down your hair' and then she would climb up to the tower—"

"And whatever her name is didn't fall out the window with somebody climbing up her hair?"

"This is a fairy tale. Wonderful things happen. Things that don't happen in real life. Let me finish. . . . One day the King's son was riding through the forest and he heard Mother Gothel command Rapunzel to let her hair down. He waited until Mother Gothel left and then went below the window and said, 'Rapunzel, Rapunzel, let down your hair for me—'"

"Don't tell me he climbed up, too."

"Yes."

"And then what?"

"They fell in love, and he asked her to be his wife—"

Caleb knelt beside me. "Forget about them." He put his hand behind my head and gently pulled me toward him. "It's you and me. Caleb and Tessa. And I didn't have to climb up your hair." He rubbed his cheek against mine, and I began to tremble.

Pulling away, he told me not to be afraid. "I wouldn't

hurt you," he said, brushing my hair from my forehead. "I'd never do that."

I pressed my face against his shoulder and closed my eyes. He held me tighter. Then he lifted my face from his shoulder and kissed me, not the way he had kissed me before. My head spun. His lips were warm and moist against mine. "Open your eyes," he said.

He smiled that wonderful smile and, at that moment, I was sure he only smiled that way for me. He kissed me again and then ran his tongue over my lips, put his hand on my breast. I began to tremble.

"Are you cold?"

I wasn't, but I nodded.

He stood, then reached down and took my hand. He wrapped the blanket around me, never taking his eyes from mine. I tried to stop the trembling, but couldn't. In the stillness I could almost hear it.

Without saying a word, Caleb guided me up the stairs, toward the top of the tower. As we climbed, the light got dimmer. Caleb put the flashlight on. Its light wound round and round as we rose to the top. Once there, some light leaked in from a small window by the tower's bell.

Caleb rummaged around on the floor until he found what he was looking for. "Here," he said, draping something around my shoulders. "I can't have you getting cold on me." He held me close, his breath rapid, his lips close to my ear. "Tessa, Tessa," he said, slowly, his voice raspy, "let down your hair for me . . . just me. . . ."

My heart vibrated through my clothes. I felt as though the blood had left my body, I was that cold. Because without looking at what he had put around my shoulders, I knew what it was. The quilt Selina and I had seen that day in the tower.

Slowly, everything began to come together. I didn't want it to. Didn't want to know all the things Selina had tried to tell me were true. Didn't want to remember how I had denied the feelings in the pit of my stomach. The day on the mower. The day in the lake. The ride on the Zipper.

I found my voice and said quietly, "I think I should go."

"Why? We're safe and snug here. Besides, it's too early."

"I feel a little sick. I'll feel better at home."

He looked out the window toward the garages and the apartment. "The whole place is as dark as a cave. You got a key?"

"Yes," I lied.

"No, you don't," he said, reaching out, putting his hand on my shoulder, sliding his hand under my blouse.

I pulled away.

"Hey, what's with you? For weeks now you've been mooning over me and now you look like a scared rabbit."

I backed up toward the stairs, but he went around me and blocked the way. "Hey," he said, "you owe me an explanation. Nobody just walks away from me."

"I just want to go home. Let me go home, Caleb. Now. Please."

"I asked you a question." He took my arm and pressed me against the wall. I couldn't get my breath. So many times I couldn't get my breath when I saw him. But this was different.

"I want to go now," I said in a tiny voice.

"You don't want to do that, Tess." He gripped my arm tighter. The expression in his eyes frightened me.

He looked at me for a long minute, then dropped my arm. "I know what's the matter," he said, his voice suddenly gentle, his eyes clouded with tears. "You think it was me, don't you? Think I was the one who got Isobel in trouble? Is that it?"

I stood still as a statue. Said nothing.

"It's a lie. I told you, it wasn't me. I just tried to help her. I swear, Tess, I didn't touch her."

I wanted to believe him so badly.

Then, as though he were in a movie and the director yelled, "Next scene," he began to punch his palm with his fist. "Do you know what this means?" He turned to me, his eyes wide, no tears visible. "I'll be shut out of the Point because of her. She's a liar, a filthy liar. She's protecting him."

He started to pace. I moved slowly toward the stairs. He stopped me. "Everyone's protecting him. You and your lousy friends. And who's going to pay for this? Me, that's who. Me."

Afraid to move, knowing I had to get out of there, something told me to talk to him, to calm him down. To tell him I understood that it would be okay. That Isobel—

"What am I supposed to do now?" he asked, pushing me harder against the wall. "Join the army? End up in Vietnam?"

I took a deep breath and hoped my voice would come. "Maybe nobody will find out. I haven't told anybody. I never will."

He backed away just a bit. "Sure. And what about that bunch of morons you hang with? You think they're not going to keep talking?"

"People know that Marie is a gossip. So is Lee Ann—"

"What about your other friend?"

"Selina? She doesn't believe Marie," I lied.

I had the urge to run toward the stairs, to get home, to get to my father. But I stood there, telling myself to keep calm, to keep talking. I thought about what my mother had said about my father, how he kept calm, didn't get emotional, how it helped people who were crazy with worry.

"You'll get into West Point." I said it softly, putting my hand on his arm.

"I have to." He started to cry. "It's what I've got to do."

"I know that. You'll go. People forget. Don't worry," I said in the softest of voices. I inched my way toward the stairs, but he took hold of my blouse.

"You're just like the rest of them. You're all alike—"

I prayed that someone would help me, prayed that I'd see my father and mother again—

"What was that?" Caleb said, looking one way and then another. "I heard something."

I willed myself to remain calm. "It was probably an owl. Or a bat. There are probably bats in here."

A loud crash came from downstairs.

"Who's there?" Caleb called out. "Who is it?"

I pulled away and ran to the stairs, Caleb after me. He grabbed my blouse again, but I started down, Caleb still holding tight. I heard my father's voice and saw him coming up to me. And then nothing.

Chapter Twenty-six

My head hurt. My whole body ached. But I felt wonderful because when I opened my eyes, my father was sitting by my bed. He had been there all night. Just like Atticus by Jem's bed.

"How do you feel?" he asked.

Afraid to trust my voice, I nodded.

He asked me to move my arms, my legs. "You took a terrible fall," he said, sitting at the edge of the bed.

"How did you know where I was?"

"Selina," he said, smoothing back my hair. "Rest awhile. I'm going to make an appointment for you with one of Dr. Nolan's colleagues." He bent down and kissed me. "It's a known fact that doctors aren't at their best when their patient is someone they love."

I started to cry.

He took my hand and rubbed it the way my mother always did.

"I'm sorry I lied."

"I know." He sighed. "Now I'm going to make you

some tea and toast. Isn't that what your mother always does?"

I nodded.

"She's coming." He checked his watch. "She's boarding just about now."

He leaned over, one hand on one side of me, one hand on the other. "Tess," he said, "things take time. Be gentle with yourself."

I reached up and held him and when I finally let go, he kissed the top of my head and went out to the kitchen to make my tea.

So many things have fallen into place about that night in the tower. How my father got there. And why? When he saw Sister Catherine that afternoon she told my father that she'd heard some things about Caleb. She had seen us together on a number of occasions and was uncomfortable with it. Hearing all of that, my father drove to Caleb's house and found out there was no party. That really shocked me, that Caleb had lied about that, too. Then Papa got in touch with Selina and she said she was almost sure he'd find us at the tower.

When we spoke, Selina asked me if I was angry with her for having done that. I told her I had prayed for it. I haven't told anybody but Selina what happened that night. She just listened;

not once did she say I-told-you-so.

I try to put it out of my mind, like my father tried to do with Vietnam. But I guess things have a way of trailing along with you, popping up when you're not even thinking about them. Probably for the rest of your life.

I think of so many things lately. How I'd wanted my father to be exactly like Atticus Finch. How foolish that was. How can anybody be exactly the way you want them? I'm not exactly the way I want me to be.

I think about how fictional characters might act when they are shut up tight on library shelves, nobody reading about them. Do they act like people when nobody is watching them? Do they behave the way the author wants them to? Or do they decide to have lives of their own, do what they want? Maybe Atticus goes off and marries Miss Stephanie. Maybe Boo Radley becomes a whole person, afraid of nothing. Like my father is trying to do.

We still walk. Most times now it's my father who calls in to me, telling me it's time. We talk, too. Some nights more than other nights. He's smoking a lot less. When I ask him when he's going to stop, I remind myself of what he told me. And

I tell him that things take time, that he's to be gentle with himself.

I think about that first day I met Caleb down at the lake. How I looked up his name in the dictionary. "Caleb, meaning dog in Hebrew, with the significance of faithful affection." How I thought its meaning was perfect for him. How I thought he was perfect and like the poetry I'd read, we would love each other till death. But now the only meaning that makes sense is the part that says, "Caleb was one of two men who survived after forty years wandering. . . ." People like Caleb do survive somehow.

I think of what I told Selina, something I know I will never tell anybody else. Some days I think it didn't happen that way, but I know it's not so. This is so hard for me to write . . . Caleb pushed me down the stairs. I wanted to believe it was one of those stupid little heels that got caught in the grate. But it wasn't. Sometimes, especially at night, I can feel the pressure of Caleb's hand on my shoulder, feel myself falling. . . .

But most of all I think of Isobel. For a long while I didn't want to believe that that same night Caleb took me to the tower, Isobel's baby was being taken from her. I could forgive his getting her pregnant, things like that happen, and even his fear of everybody finding out, and his not telling Isobel how my mother could have helped. But I can never forgive his letting her go to that place, alone, so they could take her baby. I sometimes dream about her. She is in a safe place, her baby beside her. She smiles at me and thanks me for trying to help her. She tells me she's at peace.

My mother is here now. It feels so good. We're not sure how long we're staying, but we'll be here for the rest of the summer definitely.

Selina is staying, too. She is not joining the convent. Sister Catherine said she is far too young to make a life's decision. I admire Sister Catherine for saying that. She told Selina if, when she graduates Cor Maria, she still feels the same way, they will talk about it.

It looks as if Selina might just do that, graduate from Cor Maria. Treena heard that the convent cook, ninety-two-year-old Sister Therese, was finally retiring. Treena told Sister Catherine she'd heard that Selina's mother was a fine cook. As usual, nobody can say no to Treena. Mrs. Maddox got the job. Selina is sure it won't last too long, but I told her I disagree. "Your mother wanted you to be a lady and graduate from Cor Maria, and I'll bet she'll stay to see that." Selina asked me if I meant that she'd stay until she graduated or until she became a lady. "A lady," I said. "And that will take a lifetime."

I think, too, about how lucky I am to have all the people I have in my life. My mother and father. Treena. Selina. Clio, too. And maybe one day somebody will come along and sweep me off my "petits pieds." One who will write, "Dear love, 'tis less than I have vowed but let me gather in and bring all love from earth and sea and sky. . . ." and carry me off to live happily ever after.